SNOW & THE SEVEN HUNTSMEN

A REVERSE HAREM DARK ROMANCE

ZOE BLAKE
ALTA HENSLEY

Editing by the wonderful Maggie Ryan

Cover Art by Dark City Designs

To all the dark and dirty readers, we dedicate this book to all of you.

Zoe & Alta

ONE

It was barely a sound.

The soft scrape of a boot on the floor. The rub of a shoulder against the stone wall. A muffled cough.

I was awake in an instant. Something was different. There was a tension in the air.

Throwing my covers aside, I shivered when my feet touched the icy flagstone floor. Creeping over to the high-arched windows, I parted the brocade curtains just enough to peek out. All was quiet and still. The newly fallen snow lay undisturbed, glistening and sparkling in the moonlight.

Perhaps I had imagined it?

Another sound.

This one just beyond my bedroom door.

A horrible calm settled over me as if a long anticipated storm had finally broken. I had been waiting for this day. Dreading it.

My stepmother had finally sent someone to kill me.

With my only escape route now blocked to me, I had to think fast. Pushing open the heavy curtains, I placed my hands on the black ebony frame. I once again looked over the winter scene below, the peace of a winter's eve now destroyed. My bedroom was far too high to risk a jump, but perhaps I could climb out onto the ledge and make my way to the stone balustrade of the room next door.

There was the screech of metal against metal. The scrape of a key. They were unlocking my door.

Running across the room, I picked up the small wooden spindle chair by the perpetually cold fireplace. It was one of the few pieces of furniture I was allowed in my sparse prison. Hefting it high, I raced back to the window. I hesitated. The moment I broke the window, there would be no turning back. I would have to run and keep running. I squeezed my eyes shut and smashed the chair against the glass with all my might. It shattered, sending sharp shards skittering across the floor. Grabbing the blanket off my bed, I placed it over the jagged pieces. Stepping up to the window, I tossed the remnants of the bedcovers over the sill, cutting my finger in the process. I watched in horrid fascination as three warm, crimson spots of blood fell upon the snow on the ledge, melting it.

As I gingerly stepped onto the sill, the bedroom door opened. A bitter wind cut through the threadbare fabric of my nightgown as remnants of the broken window sliced into my bare feet. With a cry, I moved onto the ledge, quickly turning to grasp the chilled stone.

Morbid curiosity getting the better of me, I peered back into the interior of my room. Looking over my shoulder, I saw three men enter, moonlight illuminating them. The brawn and bulk of their size belied their almost silent entry.

So similar they could be brothers, each was tall with broad shoulders and a harsh angular face. They wore animal skins and furs. Trophies of their past kills.

Huntsmen.

Spurred on by their fearsome looks, I dug my fingernails into the stone façade and tried to slide my foot to the right. It slipped on the ice-covered ledge. My cry of alarm echoed across the still forest, sending sleeping birds into flight.

"Well, the lass has spirit. I will give her that," said one of the men happily, a note of appreciation in his dark voice.

"Good. This would be no fun if she didn't have some fight in her," said another while clapping the first on the shoulder.

"There is no point in running. We will only hunt you down," said the third to me.

"Why have you come?" I asked.

"You know why."

I could feel all three men assessing me. No doubt, the bright moonlight was shining through my gown, leaving little to their lascivious imaginations. Was I to be used for their pleasure before they killed me? I cast a look over my shoulder to the drifts below. I could hear new voices outside, their conversation carrying across the hushed midnight landscape. More men.

"Are you going to be a good girl and come along quietly?" asked the first. With his feet planted and his arms crossed over his massive chest, he made for a foreboding sight.

"I could scream," I warned. The words came out weak and trembling as my teeth had begun to chatter from the cold.

"And no one would come to your aid."

The truth of their words sent the air rushing from my lungs. I was completely alone. The wretched irony was this conversation with my killers was the first a human being had spoken to me in years. My stepmother had ordered the servants and villagers to ignore my presence and never to speak to me almost from the moment my father had drawn his last breath. I had been wrapped in a blanket of silence and solitude for as long as I could remember.

I could feel the tears pool in my eyes. As they dropped, they froze on my chilled cheeks. "You could let me go," I whispered.

"No. We can't. You are a prize we have fought long and hard to claim. You belong to us now," explained the third man.

My brow wrinkled at his words. “You’re not here to kill me?”

A bark of laughter came from all three men.

The first one answered for the group. “You may trust us in this, lass. The very last thing we plan to do is kill you.”

“Enough talk,” ground out the second grumpily. “The others are waiting below.”

He stepped before me. Laying a hand on my chest, he pushed.

Flailing, my outstretched hands scrambled for some kind of purchase but only met with air. The sound of rushing wind tormented me as I fell backwards into nothingness. My scream lost. What was only an instant felt like an eternity.

Then...instead of the cold embrace of death, I felt warmth.

I was held in a pair of strong arms. The feel of soft fur caressed my cheek. He smelled of pine and whiskey. I looked up into his bearded face, surprised when he gave me a wink.

“Well, men. It looks like I have caught some falling Snow.”

I was surrounded by hearty laughter.

With a start, I craned my neck around. Three large burly men stared back at me with interest. Another four men.

Seven in total.

With a screech, I twisted and turned my body, trying to break free. The man who held me easily tossed me over his shoulder. I felt the heat of his large hand on the undercurve of my ass.

"You bastard!" I yelled. "Get your hands off me!"

I had a brief moment of satisfaction when I felt his hand move away. Then there was a burst of raw pain. His open palm had struck my right buttock. The thin fabric of my gown did not keep the prickling hot needles from racing over my chilled skin.

Shock kept me immobile.

One of the other men circled round my captor's back. Grabbing my dark, ebony hair, he forced my head up. I winced at the twinge of pain.

Addressing the assembled men, he said, "Let's get our new prize home so we can really begin her punishment."

I opened my mouth to scream, but he shoved a gag between my red lips, tying it tightly behind my head.

Once upon a time, I was a princess named Snow White...now, I am the captive prize of seven huntsmen.

TWO

Seven men. Seven men. Seven men.

My heart beat out a frenetic cadence as all I could think was seven men. How was I to escape from seven men?

The woods.

They were my only hope. Stealing furtive glances at them from beneath my cascade of hair, I waited for my moment. They were carrying me to a small clearing just on the other side of the castle walls.

Where were the guards?

Why was no one raising the alarm?

As we neared their horses, I could feel the muscles

in my body tense, primed for action. The very moment my bare feet touched the ground, I bolted.

Hearing their outraged shouts and cries only spurred me on.

Straining to see, the moonlight dimmed in the forest, I dodged and weaved through the dark, towering trees. Sinking deep into the icy cold slush, my feet felt cold and bruised. My palms were scraped raw as I braced myself against the rough bark of the trees to keep from slipping.

I could hear their howls of frustration as they searched the forest for me. Their large bodies crashed through the underbrush like wild beasts who had picked up the scent of vulnerable prey nearby.

Placing my back against the harsh surface of one tree, I clawed at the knot behind my head holding the gag in place. The moment the dingy fabric dropped from my lips, I sucked in a desperate breath. The frigid air stabbed at my lungs. My usually pale skin glowed a raw red as the bitter cold chafed. With nothing more than my thin silk nightgown and no protection for my feet, I would not last long exposed to the unforgiving elements.

The village was too far away, and there was no

guarantee I would find shelter and help. My only hope was to hide from the huntsmen long enough to double back to the castle. The possibility that it was my very own stepmother who had sent them after me crossed my mind. The castle would not be safe for long, but it was a massive structure with plenty of places to hide. Perhaps I could find a servant still loyal to me or my father. It was a risk I was willing to take.

Straining to hear, I was alarmed at the sudden stillness.

Something was wrong.

I could no longer hear the tread of the huntsmen's booted feet on the forest floor, or the snap of brittle tree branches as their tall frames passed. They were no longer shouting to one another or cursing my flight.

Neither was there the sound of the woodland creatures as they skittered past nor the enraged call of a bird disturbed from their slumber.

All was still.

Something was wrong.

Wincing from the piercing pain, I took a few tentative steps forward, away from the protection of the tree I was leaning on. I suppressed a grimace at the sight of my own bloodied footprints. The bitter cold had numbed my feet, but now, in addition to the cuts from the broken glass of my window, I had no doubt they were badly torn from the harsh bramble and twigs littering the forest floor. Trying to still my harsh breathing, I glanced desperately about me, searching through the darkness.

I took another step.

There was the sickening crack of splintering wood.

Something tightened around my ankle.

Screeching in pain and alarm, I was swept off my feet to hang upside down. My nightgown floated over my head, blinding me. Swinging to and fro, I struggled against the bind and the rising panic as all the blood rushed to my head.

"Freyr, looks like your snare caught a rabbit," said one of the huntsmen with an amused chuckle.

Shrieking for help, I tried to raise my body up as I fought with the fabric of my nightgown, desperate to both preserve my modesty and free my gaze.

I felt a stinging flash of burning hot pain on my buttock as someone slapped my exposed flesh.

Howling in protest, my arms flailed and punched blindly in the air.

"The princess has some spirit."

My cheeks burned with humiliation from the bawdy laughter as I dangled upside down, my legs spread indecently wide as I futilely struggled to free myself.

A heavy hand fell between my thighs, and I couldn't control my desperate sob from the overt threat of his touch. A thick finger cruelly forced its way inside my body. It felt awkward and painful as I could feel my muscles clench and tighten around the protrusion.

"She has a sweet cunny to be sure. Grabbing onto my finger like a vise. Probably tear the lass in two with one thrust from my cock."

"Well, if her cunt can't take it, we'll just have to use her ass."

"No! No! Stop!" I cried as I felt fingers grope my bottom. The tips dug between the crease and brutally pried my cheeks open. Hot tears ran down my face to dampen my hair as I felt the cool night air on my most sensitive place.

The wet tip of a finger pushed against my hidden hole.

Ignoring the pain in my ankle, my body twisted and writhed as I tried to escape their barbarous hands.

"Hold her steady, Odin."

Warm hands cupped my breasts. My nipples were painfully erect from the cold. The stranger's hands gently rolled the sensitive nubs between his fingers before brutally pinching them. I squealed in pain, but my body stilled as I tried to ease the pressure of his grip on my nipples.

"Good girl," cooed the man called Odin in a darkly soothing voice. "You will learn quickly it is better to obey."

"Please, please don't torture me so," I pleaded.

Their response was to force the finger in my bottom deeper. Sharp shocks of pain radiated through my body, causing my stomach to clench and spasm.

"I don't know, Dagr. This ass is as tight as a drum. Don't know if you'll get that tree trunk you call a cock up this one."

"I love a good challenge," was his foreboding response.

Each ruthless touch was like a brand on my chilled skin. My frantic mind could no longer focus as a fresh new horror washed over me in waves. Humiliation, pain, fear.

"Cut her down. We need to finish this."

I was held aloft in a pair of strong arms as the rope around my ankle was cut free.

"Dammit. Will you look at what she's done to her feet?"

"We'll mend her when we get to the cabin, Tore. Did you bring the boar?"

"Right here."

Watching in detached numb silence, I was too overwhelmed to react when two of the men hauled a dead wild boar into the small clearing where we stood. Taking a vicious looking knife, they sliced through the animal's tough hide. A gush of crimson red blood spilled onto the snow, the pure white blanket pristine no more. The forest was quiet with only the sickening sound of the knife cutting through bone and sinew.

"You have the box she gave us?"

"Yeah. That queen is a piece of work. Giving us the very box which contained the lass's mother's jewels, her stolen birthright, to carry the heart in."

Their words cut through my stupor. Raising my neck to peer past the arms which held me tight, I spied the enameled box. Decorated with delicate bejeweled flowers and birds, it had been a prize possession of my mother's. I watched as bloodied hands raised the lid and placed the still warm heart of the boar inside the box.

"Jerrik, take this to the queen. Tell her the deed is done. The rest of you get your horses. We need to secure our prize in case the queen becomes suspicious and wants to see the body."

The humiliation of this eve's events, coupled with the imagined horrors to come, were too much for me. I closed my eyes and surrendered to the darkness.

THREE

It felt like hours later when I opened my eyes to see a massive structure hidden deep in the woods behind the sheltering branches of several ancient pine trees.

"Here we are, princess. Your new home."

The beasts had taken me to their lair.

"Let me take a look at your feet," a huntsman said as he guided me by the arm into the cabin and sat me down on a stool near the cold hearth. Looking up at me, he added, "My name is Tore, and I handle all the wounds around here."

He wasn't asking permission, and I knew I didn't have an option, so I obediently remained on the stool. I had upset them enough with my foolish attempt at escape, and now that I was confined within the walls of the cabin with these men, I had no desire to anger my captors any further. To my right, I saw that I had left footprints of blood along the wooden floor. Tore knelt down at my feet and stared at me directly in the eyes as he did so. His dark eyes screamed of disapproval, and I couldn't maintain my eye contact for more than a mere moment due to the severity of how he looked at me. His brown shoulder-length hair hung haphazardly around his face, and a thin layer of facial hair covered his firm jaw line. With him being so close, I could smell leather and masculinity before me.

The other huntsmen seemed to go about their normal business as if this were simply another ordinary morning. A fire was lit in the hearth quickly, which I was grateful for, considering that my thin nightgown was doing very little in providing warmth.

"You shredded them up pretty badly," Tore mumbled as he held my foot in his large hand, twisting and turning it so he could get a closer look. "I'm going to need to clean the wounds and remove all the slivers."

Maybe it was because the adrenaline was wearing

off, or because Tore was actually touching my wounds, but the stinging intensified, and a dull throb emerged from the balls of my feet. I didn't want to look to see how bad they were for myself, but the growing pain told me that I had indeed *shredded them up* with my fleeing barefoot through the woods.

A huntsman whose name I had yet to hear walked up behind Tore and bent at the waist placing his hands above his knees to study my feet. "You better clean those up really good. I'll get you some hot water and a rag," he said as he looked at me with the same severe disapproval that Tore had given me. Luckily, I didn't have to endure his silent lecture for long because he walked over to a large pot of water that had just been brought in by Jerrik—who also glared at me with anger—and hung it above the now roaring fire to heat up.

Tore reached for my other foot and began pulling out the larger pieces of wood and glass that were embedded into my flesh with his fingers. For such a large man, and for someone who exuded anything but softness, he did have a gentle touch as he did so. He took great care in removing each piece with slow precision. I tried to remain as still as I could, even though I had to hiss under my breath as the sting almost became too much to bear as he did so.

"I'm sure this hurts," Tore said as he continued pulling out each invading shard of debris. For a moment, I thought I saw kindness on his stern features, but it was near impossible to read this beast of a man. He both terrified me and fascinated me at the same time. My foot looked so tiny in his hands, and I knew he could snap it in two without the least bit of effort if he truly wanted to. Yet, he handled my feet like they were one of his finest possessions, careful to never be too harsh in his movements.

I bit my lip, but refused to admit my discomfort. I always considered myself a smart woman, and running barefoot through the woods with huntsmen on horseback behind me had been far from smart. So, if having to endure in silence the removal of the forest's floor from my feet was my penance, so be it. But as agonizing minute after minute went by, I found it more and more difficult to remain still as Tore concentrated on removing every last sliver.

"Stay still," he said as he tightened his hold on my foot.

I closed my eyes and took a deep breath as I tried

to do as he commanded. I eventually opened them to see the man return with a bowl of hot water and a gray rag. The thought of having soothing water offer some relief to the burn on my feet kept me from finally breaking down and crying out for mercy.

"We could practically start a fire with all that kindling being removed from your feet," he said with a chuckle.

Tore looked up from his work for the first time and gave the man a smile. "Very funny, you dope. Can you be of some use and fetch me that salve of mine from the cabinet over there?" He pointed to a cabinet quickly, but then refocused his attention back on my feet. "It looks like I got all the splinters out. Now we just need to clean them up so we don't risk infection."

"Thank you for being so kind," I said softly.

"Do not mistake me as a kind man," Tore growled. "I tended to your injury to prevent your blood from being poisoned and you becoming ill. You are no good to any of us if you are too sick to be of any use."

I swallowed hard. Any hope of kindness from this man vanished as the heat of his gaze boring into me sent a deep and ominous chill through my body.

"Gentlemen," he said as he glanced away from me to look at the rest of the huntsmen in the main room. "Since I spent all this time fixing our broken bird who tried to fly away, I think it is only fair that I get the first turn at breaking her once again."

My heart stopped as bile built in the back of my throat. I glanced around the room as panic grew with every nod of approval from the other men. What were they agreeing to? What did Tore mean when he said he wanted to break me once again?

"That seems fair," another offered as he sat down with a large cup of ale in his hand, propping his mud-covered boots up on the wooden table. "We will all have a turn soon enough. I can be a patient man. I always believe that patience leads to happiness eventually."

"Just don't be the first to claim every part of her," Dagr said as he, too, sat down with his own ale. "Save some of her for the rest of us, and you know what part of the princess is mine."

I couldn't have protested even if I'd wanted to. Fear took hold of my body and squeezed tightly around my neck. Breath was stolen from my trembling frame as Tore effortlessly swooped me up into his arms. Being carried to his room was like being caught in a raging windstorm. Air whipped past my wayward hair, and my heart beat harder than ever next to his as he held me close—too close. I didn't have the time to take in my surroundings because all I could focus on was the large chest belonging to this beast of a man cloaked in thick leather.

Entering a smaller and sparsely furnished room, he stood me near the edge of his bed. "Remove your night dress," Tore said as if his command was as normal as any other spoken word.

I took a step back as my heart clenched. "Please... I'm...pure." I didn't want to beg, to plead, or cry for mercy since deep down I felt my doing so would only fuel the savage within these men even more.

"I would hope so," he said with a spark of humor in his eye. "Your purity is going to make this even more delicious for me."

I took another step back, only succeeding in bumping the back of my legs against the mattress.

"Remove your night dress, my broken bird." He took one step closer—the predator preparing to strike his wounded prey. He took another step.

"You can make this harder than it needs to be, but the only one who will enjoy that amount of struggle would be me. So I suggest you do as I ask."

I could see it. Feel it. There would be no mercy. There would be no kindness in this man. He had used up every last bit of decency inside of him mending my damaged feet.

I glanced toward the closed bedroom door, wondering if I had even the slightest chance of escape. But even if I somehow got around Tore's brute strength, there would be six other huntsmen waiting to have their own turns with me.

"Don't say I didn't warn you," he growled as he closed the distance between us. Before I could comprehend fully what was happening, Tore took hold of the thin material of my nightgown and ripped it right down the middle.

I tried to hold onto the pieces of fabric that barely clung to my body to preserve whatever modesty I could, but it was useless. My breasts were on full display, my sex bare before my captor, and every ounce of dignity shredded from my trembling frame.

"Ah yes, my little bird. I can see you are quite pure. Like the finest gem." He took hold of the remaining pieces of the night dress I still held between my fingertips. "A gem I plan to mar."

The sob I had somehow been holding in up until now finally escaped. I knew what was going to happen, and I also knew there was nothing I could do to stop it—Tore—from happening.

He placed his finger across my mouth, his skin rough against my quivering lips. "Shh, my bird. You don't need to cry. I promise you that you will love it. Maybe not every single moment of it, but you will eventually love it."

Shaking my head, I said, "No. No, I won't. Please."

Replacing his finger with his lips, Tore kissed me. My first kiss. The first kiss that I had sat locked away in my prison of misery fantasizing about. The dream of my childhood finally came to fruition as this man pressed his lips to mine. This was not the Prince Charming I had pictured, or even the young man stealing a quick peck behind the stable as I had often wished for. No. Not Tore. Not this man.

This man was a savage, an animal, a true huntsman who feeds off the wild.

But I was far worse than any of the beasts in this house.

For one reason alone.

I liked the kiss—God help me, I did, and I craved for more. The simple touch awoke a sensation from my deepest core. A tingle shot through me as I inhaled his essence and hungered for more. Desire sizzled in parts of my being I hadn't known existed before this very minute as Tore pushed his tongue past my partly opened lips to dance with mine.

How could I be so sinful? How could I lust after a man I barely knew? How could a simple kiss pull such powerful feelings from me?

I stood naked before a man who now ran his fingertips down my spine as he pulled me closer into a deeper kiss. His possession of my mouth was gentle, not aggressive as I had imagined it would be when he had first approached me. He was allowing me to taste him. To savor him. To appreciate and truly take in my very first kiss. No matter what was to come, this man gave me the gift of finding pleasure and joy in a first experience that I would never forget. As the kiss continued, my body hummed and lit from the inside. All the darkness of my life before this very moment seemed to vanish with the rays of light exuding from this one simple kiss. And, as though a storm was brewing in the distance, I knew the gentle touch of our lips would soon escalate, so I took this time to simply find joy.

Not wasting a moment, Tore removed his clothes as if disrobing in front of me was completely normal. As he stood nude before me, I averted my eyes so as not to invade his privacy in viewing his indecency.

"Look at me," he ordered.

I refused.

"I said, look at me."

This time, I did as he asked, and glanced his way, making certain to stare directly in his eyes and nowhere else.

"Lower. Look lower."

I swallowed hard, feeling as if his words had taken hold of my neck and squeezed.

"Yes, look lower," he said again. "Look at my cock."

Cock. Such foul language. Such scandalous demands.

I was pure.

Pure.

Why could Tore not see this for himself?

Though defying the man, and what he would do if I upset him, scared me more than staring at his *cock*.

As my heavy-lidded eyes took in the large member, hard and ready before me, Tore said, "I'm going to put that in you tonight. You know this, correct?"

My lip trembled, but I nodded. There was no sense in fighting the inevitable. My fate had been sealed the minute the huntsmen stole me away.

Without waiting another second, Tore pushed me back onto the bed and ran circles along the heated flesh of the curve of my belly, dipping his hand lower between my legs. His fingers ran along my silky folds, spreading the wetness encountered all over my cunny. Humiliation washed over me and I tensed, attempting to clamp my legs together to conceal my arousal.

What must he think of me? What kind of woman allows the demon of lust to come so easily?

He removed his hand from between my clenched thighs and spanked the top of my mons. "Do not try to hide from me." He dipped his finger back to my soaking sex when I spread my legs in surprise from the quick slap. "It pleases me to see that my touch has this effect on you." He moved his finger to my little pearl and caressed it ever so gently.

I bucked up, surprised by such a powerful sensation.

The hunger in his eyes practically changed his appearance. He seemed predatory; so different than the man who'd tended to my feet only a short time ago.

Heat radiated over my body, the crux between my legs throbbing in need. No matter how much I tried to resist, I couldn't fight the sensations of desire. The feeling of his hand on my most private of parts was most indecent, yet so tantalizing. Taking a moment to breathe deeply and try to gain some control of my licentious body, I waited in anticipation of what I already knew would come.

Tore spread my legs wide, watching the seam of my womanhood open for him. My tiny hole had never before been entered, but Tore maintained control and went slowly. Running his finger along each side of my delicate petals, he soaked up my juices with his fingertip, coating the opening to my entrance nice and well. With as much care as he could, he pressed his wet finger past my opening and eased his way in.

I gasped and tensed, but then relaxed when Tore slowly began to move his finger in and out of my tight channel. He leaned down and kissed my thatch of little black curls, inhaling the musky scent of my out of control desire.

"Relax, my little bird," he coaxed as his finger glided in and out. "I need to get this sweet cunt of yours ready for me. I'm not a small man, and I don't want to hurt you...too much."

When my legs relaxed back open and my hips thrust up to meet his mouth, silently begging for more of his kisses, he whispered, "That's my good girl. Let me prepare you to become mine in all ways."

His tongue flicked my sensitive nub, nipping it between his lips. My hands ran up both sides of his head, driving his face into the most forbidden part of my body as my moans intensified.

"Tore...Tore? This feeling. I feel..." Panic laced my words. I didn't know what to think about the sensations flooding in. I had never...I had never... "Tore!"

My head thrashed side to side, and my breathing became ragged.

"Come for me, Snow. Fill my mouth with your sweet cream. Release."

My hips bucked as my moan turned into a tiny scream. My cunny quivered around his mouth, and I knew the taste of my release coated his tongue. He lapped up every last bit of my completion as my body shook on the tail end of my climax.

As if not wanting my body to fully become sated, Tore moved up to my breasts and began to circle his tongue around one nipple, and then moved to pay the same attention to the other. He molded the flesh of my firm and perky mounds with his hands.

Stretching up, he placed his lips at the shell of my ear and whispered, "I'm going to put my cock inside of you now. It will hurt a little, but I will try to make it as easy as possible."

Placing the head of his cock at my entrance, he slowly eased in. I knew this was the time where he fully claimed me. "Take a deep breath and relax," he ordered as he pushed firmly against my opening, spreading me wide as I cried out when a pop occurred deep within my core. "Shhh…" he cooed as he paused for a moment so I could adjust to his girth.

After a few moments, he launched a steady rhythm

of pushing in and out, while placing soft kisses along the side of my neck. In a steady staccato, his cock pulled out just enough to spread my opening, and then plummeted back inside so deep I could feel his cock push up against where the inside of my heated sex ended. In and out, he claimed me. In and out, I gave myself to him.

The huntsman.

Tore smiled as he pressed his lips to mine. "Good. Very, very good."

He positioned his body so he was driving his hardness into my pulsating pussy before my climax was over. His thrusting continued the frenzy. Driving the orgasm to a new level, Tore claimed me with a fervor like nothing I could have envisioned. My body melted into his. My core clung to his wanton energy. Plunging deeper, Tore's hardened length stretched my tight cunny to the maximum. My sex stung, my body ached, but euphoria conquered all.

Tore flipped me over onto my stomach in one fluid motion. He pulled my hips up so I was positioned on all fours. His roughened palm pressed between my shoulder blades, causing my upper body to rest against the bed. My bare buttocks were now up and angled in full display

"The most beautiful sight I have ever seen," he praised. "You are far more than just a broken bird."

The sexual beast inside was breaking through my body, smothering any control that remained. I wanted Tore back inside of me. I wanted it hard, I wanted it rough, and I wanted Tore to continue to take my body with uncontrolled abandon.

He grabbed my hip with one hand and a handful of hair with the other. His cock impaled me with a force that made me scream. He pulled my hair back as he drove in and out with a carnal need. Releasing the grip of my hip, he spanked my bottom. Not like a punishment but a spank of pure erotic pleasure. He continued to spank while driving his hardness deep within.

"Listen to me well, broken bird. Never disobey any of the huntsmen, or you will get far worse than what I am doing here. You are to be submissive, obedient, and compliant in all the ways we ask." Tore continued the stinging slaps against my burning behind. I gasped with each reminding blow. "Some of my fellow huntsmen are not forgiving or tolerant men. Remember this warning."

I arched my back further. The electricity from the

spanking only enhanced the approaching orgasm returning to my body. “Yes, sir.”

He grabbed both of my hips with his hands as he pushed and pulled his cock within my warm depths. His breathing sped, his moans increased. I screamed as the orgasm rocked through my body with more force than before. Tore thrust as deeply as possible as he called out my name while spilling his seed into my awaiting womb.

FOUR

I awoke to the sound of laughter.

After a lifetime spent waking to cold, unfeeling silence, it felt strangely comforting. Pulling the heavy quilt over my shoulder, I curled up onto my side, closed my eyes and listened.

The harsh clang of metal. The scrape of a fork on a plate. Muffled conversation. The heavy thump of footsteps.

Life. Humanity.

Burying my face in the blankets, I hid a smile. It was ludicrous really. These were common sounds in kitchens across the land and yet, they swept over me like music. After being shackled with only my own meager thoughts for company, day after day, month after month, year after year, the break from isolation was thrilling. How odd that these quaint sounds of domesticity should come from these large, beastly men—my abductors. Yet, by stealing my freedom, they were setting me free. Free from a crushing solitude.

As I laid secure in my cocoon, I heard my name. Sitting up, I strained to hear. Was it Tore? Would he relate to his fellow huntsmen my humiliation? How despite my struggle, my body betrayed me in the end? Would he regale them with the story of my cries and moans? How I spread my legs and practically begged him to hurt me more? My cheeks burned at the thought. Reaching between my legs, I cupped my cunny, the soreness another reminder of his brutal taking of my maidenhood and my shameless response.

Still, there was no denying his raw savagery was tempered with a harsh, almost reluctant, kindness. Wiggling my toes, I was surprised to feel no tightness or pain. The salve Tore had used on my bruised and cut feet had done much to heal the wounds.

Brushing away a tear, I tried to focus. Hiding behind a false sense of normalcy, no matter how inviting those sounds may be, no matter his show of kindness with my feet, would not help me in my current predicament. The reality was, I had been taken from one prison to another. There was no doubt in my mind my stepmother was behind the deed. These huntsmen would have no reason to lie to me. Even if I wanted to escape back to the castle, what would be the point? I would either be killed the moment I crossed the gate or worse—imprisoned even deeper inside the castle walls. Tossed in a cell, perhaps the dungeon even, until all my father's subjects had forgotten my very existence...if they hadn't already.

My stepmother's tale of my madness and cruelty to myself and others had hit their mark. Even servants once loyal to me and my plight had begun to doubt my sanity as the years stretched on...not that I blamed them. It was a compelling story. The poor princess driven mad by her father's death. What a sympathetic creature my stepmother must be! The woman forced to care for the mad daughter of her dead husband. Reluctantly taking on the role of sovereign since my weak mind would not allow me to rule. My, she played that role well. No one ever questioned it. No one ever thought that perhaps, just perhaps, she had stolen my birthright.

Bitterness rose in my throat like bile. Bitterness

and regret. How could I have let my grief blind me to her machinations? How could I have believed a woman who had never shown me an ounce of kindness or a soft word while my father was alive would suddenly care for my well-being? That I actually believed her when she said she was giving me time and space to grieve! That I had never questioned her as she slowly usurped the throne which was rightfully mine. The cruel truth was I was as responsible for my own imprisonment as if I had turned the key in the lock myself.

And now I was alone…I had no coin, no friends or even clothes.

What was I to do now? Escaping while my feet were still healing seemed futile and dangerous. I would never survive for long on my own. I needed to bide my time and wait. Surely there would be another opportunity to escape when I was more prepared.

Or perhaps the huntsmen were the answer? Perhaps instead of my damnation they could be my salvation? If I somehow gained their loyalty and trust, maybe they would consent to helping me. Help me to do what was the question. Overthrowing my stepmother would take more than seven huntsmen, no matter how large and skilled at hunting they may be. Did I even want the throne? It had done nothing but cause strife and misery for my father. He was never able to do anything he truly wanted, always constrained by duty and responsibility. The crown yet another form of imprisonment.

I had been adrift so long in isolation with no hope of a future that I now had no idea what it was I truly wanted.

Unbidden, my mind returned to the previous night, in this very bed. The way Tore forced me beneath him. He'd not only forced my body to respond but my mind as well. Forced me to actually *feel* something, breaking through the blank numbness that had crept over my existence.

It had been a terrifying, exhilarating rush. To *feel* again!

Anger, fear, pain, passion. I'd consumed it all like a woman starved.

That was what I wanted...at least for now. To *feel* again.

Later. When I had drunk and eaten my fill, when I was sated on emotion, when my senses no longer felt cumbersome and unused...then I would think of the future...of a plan...of escape.

The sound of my name broke through my wandering thoughts again.

My stomach clenched as I crept out of the bed, gingerly putting weight on my still bruised feet. Sparing a glance for my ripped nightgown on the floor, I shifted the blanket higher over my shoulders to cover my bare frame. Dragging the quilt with me, I stole toward the railing which overlooked the hall.

The huntsmen's home was an enormous cabin with a central hall built around a massive stone structure—a fire pit. Gray and brown rounded stones, carefully placed, formed a circular chimney to capture the smoke. Over the fire was a wrought iron roasting spit, laden with some form of game from the huntsmen's endeavors. Around the open fire pit were cushioned benches.

On one end was the kitchen with another smaller enclosed fireplace for baking, and at the other end was a rough-hewn oak dining table with over a dozen chairs. The entire space resembled an ancient Viking hall which seemed fitting in my mind. On the second level were their rooms, each reached from a walkway which encircled the hall.

I knelt on the hard wooden floor and tried to overhear the conversation below.

"More. She needs more," said one of the huntsmen, I had no idea which.

"Are you sure she can handle it?" asked another.

Good god. Forgetting my resolve to experience emotion and life for a change, I recoiled. They couldn't possibly mean more of what Tore had done to me last night? I didn't think I could handle much more...what if...oh god...what if they meant more...of them? More than one in my bed at a time. Good god! Was that even possible?

"She needs it," said another.

"You're right."

I recognized that voice. It was Tore. After last night, I didn't think I would ever forget the sound of his growled commands and deep moaning.

"She is nothing but skin and bones. That fucking witch must have been starving the poor girl to death, hoping she would die and solve all her problems," continued Tore.

I was taken aback by the hatred and venom in his voice...and on my behalf.

"Tore's right. Steen, add more butter...and don't be stingy on the boysenberry preserves either."

These gruff and scary men were talking about...my breakfast?

With renewed resolve, I rose. Wrapping the blanket more tightly around my body, I hesitantly took a step toward the main staircase which would lead down into the hall.

They turned at the sound of my descent. With a wry smile, I couldn't help but think what a rag-tag mockery of a queen I must look like as I slowly walked down the stairs, trailing my colored quilt of a cloak, all eyes on me.

And what a queen's court these gruff men made with their wild hair, hard glares and fur-wrapped frames.

A court of beasts. Shuddering, I despaired of my earlier thoughts. How could I be so foolish to think that I could tame these men? The idea that I could possibly convince them to join my side against my stepmother was the naïve dream of a little girl still hoping for a Prince Charming.

"So she has arisen," said one of the huntsmen as he bent low, the very picture of a proper courtier bowing.

Tightening my fist on the blanket as I clutched it close to my breast, I didn't know how to respond.

"It's Odin," he offered helpfully.

"Odin," I whispered with a slight nod of my head. Odin. The one with the light brown hair tied back into a small queue with a piece of dark rawhide.

If I was going to be among these men for the foreseeable future, I would definitely need to learn all of their names.

Accepting his offered hand, I allowed him to lead me to one of the benches before the fire.

Another placed a plate of food on my lap.

"Dagr," he stated helpfully without my having to ask. Dagr. The tallest one with the cobalt blue eyes.

As I was trying to form the words to thank him, my eyes captured the gaze of Tore from across the room. He gave me a knowing wink. Feeling my cheeks heat, I concentrated on the food before me. It was a piece of toasted bread slathered with fresh butter and preserves. After years of being served, at best, cold grizzled meat with a mug of stale beer as my morning meal, it looked heavenly.

Careful to keep the blanket over my bare shoulders, I eased my hand out from beneath its folds to pick up the bread. Ignoring all the curious gazes on me, I bit into it with relish. I was unable to suppress a groan as the creamy butter mixed with the tart sweetness of the preserves and the warm, comforting taste of the crusty bread flooded my mouth. Closing my eyes, I flicked my tongue out to capture a dollop of butter before taking another bite. Lost in the sheer bliss of savoring this sweet treat, it took me a moment to realize I was the subject of their intense scrutiny. Opening my eyes, I watched as several of the men shifted in their seats. At least two awkwardly cleared their throats as another rose, his hands going to his belt.

"None of that," commanded Odin. "We have to check the traps and track that buck Dagr spotted earlier this morn. There will be plenty of time for amusement after our work is done."

Amusement? Was I the source of their amusement? Judging from the hungry looks they were all giving me, I felt as if I were the sweet morsel being offered up on a plate!

"Leave the lass alone. After a night spent with Tore between her legs, her pussy will tear like cheap silk if one of us tries to have a go at her, right now."

Cringing at his crude language, I couldn't suppress an indignant glare. The huntsman who'd spoken was the one who had carelessly tossed me over his shoulder and spanked my bottom when I dared to cry out or wiggle to escape. Yes, I might not yet know his name, but I knew the man.

"Gather your gear men, we leave soon. Jerrik, show the lass the kitchen and explain her duties."

Jerrik had the greenest eyes I had ever seen. They were like bright, polished emeralds and seemed to dance with some secret amusement.

"Follow me, Snow."

I couldn't help but cast a despondent look toward my plate with my half-eaten piece of bread.

Sensing my distress, the one I heard them call Steen, took the plate from my lap. "You can finish this after we leave."

Securing the blanket around me, trying not to trip, I followed Jerrik across the great hall. The wood planked floor was surprisingly warm on my bare feet.

"It will be your duty to prepare our meals. We will be back in a few hours and will expect a warm meal and ale to be ready and waiting. Do you understand?" asked Jerrik.

Good god! Cook? I had never cooked anything in my life. What was I going to do? I wasn't sure what would happen if I told them the truth. Worried they may find me useless and not worth the trouble, I just stayed silent.

"You can cook?"

I nodded yes, still refusing to speak as I glanced through the window over his shoulder at the thick layer of icicles which clung to the frame, hoping they would not discard me out into the icy, winter morn when they learned I could not prepare meals like a proper female ought.

Odin gave my blanket a disgruntled look. "How is she supposed to cook clutching this damn blanket? Did we think to grab clothes for her?"

"What does she need clothes for?" asked Freyr with a wicked gleam to his eye.

Taking a step back, my shoulders rounded as I wrapped my arms tightly around me. Were they really going to force me to appear before them all, bare without the protection of clothes?

"Be reasonable, Freyr. She'll catch a chill and be of no use to any of us," groused Steen.

"Good point. I'll fetch her some linens of mine," offered Dagr as he bounded up the staircase. His long powerful stride took the stairs three at a time.

"Grab her a pair of woolen stockings to protect her feet as well," called out Tore.

Dagr returned with a cream linen shirt, a leather belt and a pair of gray wool stockings.

They all took a step toward me. I tried to step back, but my legs became entangled in the trailing blanket.

"Drop the blanket, Snow."

Panic rose in my breast as the large men formed a circle around me, trapping me. Their coarse attire of fur and leather gave them the appearance of a pack of wolves, ready to pounce.

"I…I…I could just change in one of the rooms," I responded weakly as I became lightheaded with fear. Clutching the blanket so close, I could feel my nails tear.

They all slowly shook their heads. Seven pairs of dark, unsympathetic eyes stared down at me.

The cold eyes of predators.

"We have explained this to you, Snow. You are ours now. You will either obey Magni and drop the blanket, or face the consequences." This from Dagr. Standing closest to me, I could feel the threatening rumble of his words.

"Please...I can't—"

"We are losing patience, Snow," warned Magni.

Defeated, I lowered my head. Keeping my eyes averted, I slowly loosened my grip on the blanket. Feeling its heavy protective weight slide off my shoulders, I bit my lower lip to keep from crying out. Humiliation coiled and twisted my stomach into knots as I could feel their eyes on me. A finger was placed under my chin, forcing my head up. I met the gaze of Dagr. The back of his knuckles skimmed the upper curve of my breast as he caressed my bare stomach with the fabric from the shirt he held.

Unable to tear my gaze from his, I reached out blindly for the covering. As soon as the bunched fabric was in my hand, I hastily pulled it over my head, grateful for the meager covering the thin, coarse linen provided as its ample folds fell almost to my knees.

Dagr took a step forward. Reaching around me, he placed his thick leather belt around my waist. I gasped as he pulled the strap through the thick buckle and pulled it tight. Leaning down, he whispered into my ear, "Keep this nice and warm for me until I can use it on your bare ass."

My mouth fell open in shock. Did he really mean to punish me with the very belt around my waist? I couldn't suppress a shiver of awareness. The leather felt heavy and tight as it rested on my slim hips. A constant, constrictive warning of my new position as their captive.

A warm hand caressed my calf. Tore knelt before me. He was lifting my foot to place one of the wool stockings on.

"I can do—"

"Silence," responded Tore as he ran his large palm up higher, cupping the undercurve of my bare bottom.

Without thinking, I reached out to grab Dagr's strong arm for support as my knees threatened to buckle. I raised my other foot, allowing Tore to run his hand possessively up my exposed leg as if he had the right to touch me so intimately. But then, hadn't he taken that right last night?

Had it been *taken* or *given*? My heart beat faster at the disturbing thought.

Dressed in my strange attire that both protected and exposed me to their gaze, I crossed my arms over my chest, painfully aware you could see the hard buds of my nipples pressing against the shirt.

The men chuckled in response. Amused by my modesty.

"Remember to have our meal ready upon our return," warned Jerrik as he hefted a bow onto his shoulder.

"What if the lass tries to escape?" asked Magni.

Grabbing a fistful of my hair to get my attention, Dagr hissed, "Then we hunt her down like a doe and bring her back here...to punish for her disobedience."

"I promise. I won't try to escape. I have nowhere to go!" I pleaded. Whether I was more alarmed by their threats or just desperate to please my new captors...I couldn't say. I did know I was telling the truth. I had already determined escape would be foolhardy until I could secure supplies and give my feet at least another night to heal. For better or worse, the dangerous huntsmen were my best bet for survival—at least for now.

They left without saying another word. I didn't dare even walk toward the door for fear they were still watching me. Instead, I walked over to the kitchen area.

Somehow, I needed to learn how to cook within

the next few hours or face the wrath of seven angry, hungry huntsmen.

I tried to think back to before my mother died, when the castle was still a warm and inviting place. I remembered spending my afternoons as a child in the kitchens, pestering the cook for a treat. Thinking back to what I had seen, it didn't seem so hard. I remembered the cook always calling out for flour and butter. That's where I would start!

Searching the various bins and cupboards, I found some white powder which looked like flour. The butter was already on the large wooden slab which served as a work space. Grabbing a bowl, I poured some flour from the sack into it, coughing as a cloud of dust surrounded me. Taking a wooden spoon, I scooped a section of butter and added it to the flour. Stirring only seemed to coat the hunk of butter with flour. Odd. When cook had done this, it had seemed to make a thick, creamy mixture. I must be missing something. Removing the cheesecloth from an earthenware jug, I inhaled the spicy, earthy scent of mustard. Perfect! Tipping the jug over my bowl, I poured the entire contents into my flour mixture. Taking up my spoon, I vigorously stirred until the flour blended with the mustard and butter.

Behind me was a small iron stove. Using a discarded piece of cloth, I carefully opened the door, squinting as a rush of dry heat hit my face. Inside, the logs glowed orange with slashes of coal black. The bowl must just sit within the flames. Shrugging my shoulders, I placed the bowl on top of the embers and closed the stove door.

Cooking was easy.

❄

THICK BLACK SMOKE poured from the oven. With shaking hands, I grabbed the jug of ale from nearby and tossed the liquid into the stove. There was an awful hiss, then the smoke billowed from the stove once again…thicker and blacker.

My eyes stung as I swiveled around, trying to get my bearings. The hall was obscured behind a wall of smoke. Stretching my arms out, I took a step forward, then another.

I could hear indistinct shouting.

I took another blind step forward and collided with something warm and solid.

“I’ve got her,” bellowed Jerrik.

Strong arms wrapped around my shoulders as I

was lifted off my feet and carried out into the cold bright sunshine.

I watched as Tore followed him carrying a smoking bowl of burnt sludge. He tossed the smoldering mess into the nearest snow bank.

Hiding my face in Jerrik's shoulder, I tried to avoid the angry lecture...or worse...that I knew was coming.

As Jerrik held me aloft, each of them shouted over the other.

"...could have been killed."

"Punished for..."

"....burned down the cabin."

"Of all the imbecilic..."

"Punished..."

"Lied about..."

"Get the belt..."

"Punished..."

Out of the cacophony of bellows, exclamations and shouts...the only word I kept hearing over and over again was...*punished.*

FIVE

"Where are you taking me?"

Magni stayed silent.

After the chaos of my kitchen disaster, Magni tossed a large fur over my shoulders and lifted me onto the back of his horse. With a curt nod to the other huntsmen, he set off into the woods.

Through the dark crooked branches of the trees, I could see the dying purple and orange flames of the sun as it set, casting the woods into shadow. Still we continued...deeper and deeper into the dark forest. The only sound was the crunching of the snow beneath the horse's hooves.

Finally, the trees thinned, and we came upon a clearing.

I had never seen anything like it before in my life. Curls of steam rose above the crystal blue waters of a large pool. It was surrounded by massive ice-covered boulders.

"What is this place?" I asked in awe.

"A warm spring," responded Magni curtly as he lowered me down from his horse. Despite the wet snow creeping through my wool socks, I could not resist stepping closer to the warm pool of water. Leaning over a boulder, I gazed down into its depths. The water was so clean and clear you could see straight down to the bottom. Expecting to see mud and sediment, I was surprised to see nothing but smooth rock. It was if the entire pool had been carved out of the very rock which protected it.

"All right, lass, take off your clothes."

I swung back to face Magni. The shirt Dagr had given me earlier was now grimy with black soot, but something was better than nothing.

"If I have to ask one more time, I will take that belt from around your waist and put it to good use."

Knowing full well he would make good on his threat, I reluctantly pulled at the belt buckle which secured the voluminous folds of the shirt around my small waist. Letting it fall to the ground, I started to play with the buttons down the front. Magni's sigh of frustration was my only warning before he marched up to me and swept the shirt over my head. With a cry, I bent my knees as I curled my body forward trying to protect myself both from the cold and his even colder gaze.

"Into the pool," he demanded.

I gingerly stepped up to a small space between the boulders. Slipping off my now wet stockings, I placed a foot in the water, testing it. It felt wonderfully warm. Cooler than bathwater but still pleasant. Forgetting my modestly, I eagerly stepped further into the warm spring until I could feel the soothing water lap at my shoulders.

So lost in the blissful moment, I forgot about Magni's presence till I heard a splash behind me.

Turning, I saw his naked form as he walked toward me. The water made his progress slow and exaggerated. I could see his body through the clear blue water...I could see *all* of him.

Good god. His member jutted out large and thick.

With a start, I tried to swim backwards, away from his threatening approach.

Magni grabbed my flailing legs and pulled me

back, pressing my back against his front. I could feel the press of his cock against my skin. His body was warmer than the water which surrounded us.

I winced as my neck was forced back by his grip on my hair.

"You were a very bad girl today."

"I didn't do it on purpose," I pleaded.

"You put yourself in danger by lying to us. You should have told us you had no talent in the kitchen, lass. The whole damn cabin could have burned down around your ears."

"I know! I know. I'm sorry."

"You will be. Lying to us is not acceptable. I'm going to teach that pretty mouth of yours a lesson."

Magni turned me to face him. Grabbing my chin, he caressed my lower lip.

"You're going to open these sweet lips of yours and swallow my cock."

Shaking my head no, I tried to move out of his grasp.

Gripping me by the shoulders, he pulled me forward till my breasts were crushed against his hard chest.

"No is not an option."

Using his grip on my shoulders, he forced me beneath the water. Without thinking, I opened my mouth to scream as my legs kicked and flailed.

Magni wrenched me above the surface. Sputtering water, my hair in my eyes, I opened my mouth to suck in a ragged, desperate breath. He forced me under again.

As I struggled against his grip, his cock brushed my cheek. Bracing my hands against his thighs, I tried to push off from him. His grip loosened on my shoulders. I swiveled my body and tried to kick off with my legs to swim to safety on the other side of the pool, but there was no escape.

Magni fisted his hand in my long, black hair and pulled me back to the surface by my own locks.

I screamed with all my might. The only response I heard was the echo of my own cries as they bounced off the surrounding rocks.

"Struggle all you want, but you *will* suck my cock."

I twisted and turned, my hands clawing at his wrist, trying to dislodge his grip on my hair.

Once again, he forced me beneath the water, this time quickly raising me to the surface. I was only given a moment to suck in one desperate gulp of air before I was forced under again.

With his grip on my hair, he forced my head between his legs. Knowing I had no choice, I opened my mouth and felt the warm length of his cock slip between my lips. I choked as water slipped down my throat. His only response was to force my head forward, impaling my mouth on his shaft.

My lungs started to seize. They felt like they were on fire. Instinctively, I knew he would not allow me to surface unless I did as I was told. Desperately, I moved my mouth up and down his hard length like I thought he wanted as his hand guided my head forward and back.

I felt a harsh tug on my hair as he pulled me to the surface. My arms splashed wildly about as I coughed and sputtered.

"This time, I won't let you up to breathe until you take it to the hilt. I want to feel the back of your throat tighten around the head of my cock," he growled.

"No!" I cried out. I was only able to grab a quick gasp of air before I was forced under the water again. I could see the dark curls of hair on his chest before I was once again forced in front of his jutting cock.

My legs floated out behind me as I grabbed onto his hips for purchase. Opening my mouth, I tried to force myself onto his cock. The thick weight pressed against my tongue. My shoulders shuddered as I suppressed the urge to gag. My jaw ached. As air escaped through my nose, the bubbles tickled my face. I could feel my hair as it floated about my shoulders, brushing my cheeks.

Still I pressed on.

Using my grip on his hips, I pulled forward. My body floated toward his. I forced his cock deep, but I couldn't take it. My stomach clenched. I started to gag as his shaft pressed against the back of my throat. The bottom of my tongue was scraped raw by the sharp edge of my teeth. In a panic, I tried to push off.

Magni placed his hand against the back of my head and pushed me the final few inches. I tried to scream around his cock, the sound only a few futile bubbles escaping the corners of my mouth. I could feel his shaft as it lodged down my throat column. His hips moved forward as my nose was crushed against his stomach.

Desperately, I started to kick and punch.

I was out of breath. My chest constricted.

In the last moment, Magni relented. Gripping my hair, he brought me to the surface. I clung to his shoulders as I sucked in air.

"Swallow it."

Was all I heard before I was once again surrounded by the eerie silence under water. I couldn't even hear my own screams. With a sob, I opened my lips and felt the hard length of his cock force its way into my mouth. Magni began to thrust his hips as I was forced to accept him deep down my throat.

After several thrusts, I was allowed to rise to the surface on my own.

The icy cold air tore at my sore throat as I heaved and sputtered.

His strong hands landed on my shoulders. This time instead of forcing me under the water, he spun me around till my back was facing him.

His hands moved down my body before gripping my thighs just above the knees. Pulling up, he forced my feet out from under me. My body pitched forward. My arms flailed, splashing against the surface as I struggled to keep my head above the water. He pulled back on my legs till I could feel his hips between my thighs. My furious kicks did nothing to dislodge his skillful grip. I could feel the hard push of his cock along the seam of my ass.

My struggle intensified but with my legs forced to straddle his hips, I could not kick out. My body dipped below the surface of the water.

Once again, I felt his fist in my hair as his cock pushed against my still sore cunny. My body was floating straight out in front of his own. I could feel his free hand span my hip to steady me before his heavy cock thrust forward.

My scream was a cascade of bubbles as my arms struck and thrashed at the water.

My body burned as it struggled to accept the width of his cock. It felt like he was tearing me in two.

My head stung as he wrenched me above the water by my hair. My body bowed backwards. As I sucked in a needed breath, the position forced my hips back, pushing his cock further inside of me.

He lowered me beneath the crystal blue surface again.

I no longer had the energy to struggle.

I gave in to the power of his grip.

My body floated free.

He began to fiercely pound into me, stretching my tight inner passage.

Then something shifted…changed.

The heavy, languid feeling of floating, of having my senses muted by the water allowed me to truly experience every sensation. I could feel the rhythmic pace of his thrusts. His fingers as they dug into my flesh. The caress of the water against my skin.

My body started to respond as my mind began to lose its grip on reality. I felt lightheaded…dizzy and unfocused.

Still he thrust.

I opened my mouth as if to breathe but only experienced the slightly metallic taste of the mountain spring water.

The pain twisted and spun into pleasure as I felt dominated, overwhelmed. Magni controlled everything…the very breath in my body. The pressure began to build. I could feel it everywhere. In my lungs, between my legs. There was a rushing pounding sound echoing in my ears which matched his thrusting cock. Everywhere there was pressure.

To find a release.

To breathe.

The very moment I felt as though death was upon me, Magni raised my body out of the water with a roar. His arm slashed across my front, holding me upright against his chest. My knees squeezed tightly into his sides. The pressure of my own weight forced my body down his shaft, fully impaling me on his cock.

The pleasure of air rushing into my body violently collided with the bliss of my release.

I wasn't sure how long we remained intertwined within each other's arms, but reality sank in when Magni wrapped my shaking body with fur as he held me close. It was not the cold air which caused me to shiver. I was struck dumb by the intensity of the experience. With my mind unable to cope or form the words for what had just happened, all the energy, all the anger, all the passion and fear left my body quivering in awareness.

Exhausted, the gentle rocking of his horse lulled me to sleep in his arms as he took me back to the cabin.

SIX

"We have to go to town to sell the furs," Tore announced. "And to pick up some fresh provisions."

"We also have the dry meat that will sell," Dagr added.

I stood silently near the fire, acting as if I wasn't paying close attention to what the men were discussing, even though a surge of hope almost made my knees go weak. Would they go to town without me? Leave me behind again? I knew the nearest town was far enough away, and that them being gone could give me the perfect opportunity to finally plan and execute my escape. Sufficient time had passed that my feet had healed enough that I felt confident that I could run again.

My heart fell when I heard Freyr say, “You all go to town to do that. My brother and I will remain back and watch over Snow.”

“Yes, we’ll stay,” Steen agreed, kicking off his boots as he leaned back in the large wooden chair by the kitchen table.

There would be no way for escape if I had the twins watching over me. No way at all. Defeat darkened the small spark of light that had been present for the quick moment.

Taking hold of a rag, I began wiping down the surfaces around the kitchen, trying to not show my emotions or the fact that I was trying to come up with a million ways to flee during this small window of opportunity the huntsmen going into town afforded me.

There had to be a way.

I nodded politely in silent goodbye as the huntsmen—other than Freyr and Steen—set out to leave, wondering if it would be the last time I would see any of them again.

When the door finally closed, I heard Freyr say, “I’m sleepy. I’m going to go rest for a bit.”

I turned with hope in my heart to see Steen nod

with a roll of his eyes. "You go ahead, you lazy arse. I'm going to go collect some firewood. Someone better do the work around this place."

I walked over to the broom propped up in the corner, hoping that I appeared to be simply lost in my chores rather than masterminding my escape. If either of them grew suspicious, I knew I would lose what could be my one and only chance at finally breaking away from my cage guarded by these wolves.

Luckily, it appeared as if both brothers had no idea of the plans running through my head because Freyr stood and walked to his bedroom while Steen exited the house with an ax in his hands. The minute the door closed, I jumped into action. I knew I didn't have long. Running to the front door, I reached for a pair of leather boots that belonged to one of the huntsmen and put them on my bare feet. They were far too big but would be better than attempting to run through the woods barefoot again. The borrowed shirt I wore wouldn't be enough to keep me warm, so I grabbed a fur and threw it over my shoulders. It was heavy, oversized, and smelled musty, but it would certainly keep me warm in the woods. I paused for a moment and considered grabbing a satchel of food, but worried that Freyr would decide against taking a nap, or Steen would come back having forgotten something. There was no time to pack, and I would just have to hope I could find food or even some kind villager who would assist me.

Opening the door, my heart beat hard against my chest.

This was my chance. My only chance.

Run. Run fast.

Charging forward with all my courage helping give me the strength, I ran straight into a stone wall.

Or what felt like a stone wall.

Looking up into the eyes of a furious Steen, I gasped in surprise.

"What are you doing?" He looked down at the oversized boots, then the fur, and then into my wide eyes. "Were you trying to run away again?"

"No, I…I needed to…"

"Don't lie to me," he boomed.

Rather than trying to come up with a futile excuse, I bolted to the right and ran as fast as the ill-fitting boots would allow me to. Maybe Steen wouldn't chase me. Maybe he would allow me to go and just pretend he didn't see me in the first place. Maybe—

No.

Steen took hold of the nape of my neck and forcibly pulled me back against his chest mid-run. My body snapped back, and had it not been for his thick arms holding onto me, I surely would have fallen to the muddy ground.

"Fool," he hissed as he dragged me into the house. "Such a fool you are." He almost sounded sorry for me as he said the last sentence. "Freyr!" he called out as we crossed the threshold. "Freyr, get out here."

As if disturbing the grizzly bear from hibernation, Freyr emerged from his room with a furrowed brow and clenched jaw. "This better be important," he said as he walked down the stairs. The sight of the fur on me, as well as the borrowed boots revealed the story of what would soon be the reason for my demise before Steen even needed to say the words.

"I caught her trying to flee," Steen informed as he pushed me fully into the house.

Freyr didn't need to yell or bellow out his fury. His eyes revealed it all. "Take her to my room. Now! It's high time we teach this runaway a lesson to assure she never does something like this again."

"I'm sorry," I blurted. "I truly am. There will be no need to teach me anything. You are right. I shouldn't have tried to escape again. I don't know what got into me."

"Take her to my room," Freyr repeated as he ran the palm of his hand over his face, rubbing away any last bit of sleep from his features. "There's rope under my bed. Tie her up."

As Steen took hold of my arm to do as his brother asked, I tried to pull away. "You don't need to do that."

"Come on," Steen said as he pulled me toward Freyr's lair. "You did this to yourself."

When we crossed the threshold of the room, I spun on my heels to look at him. "Please, Steen. I know I shouldn't have tried to escape. But it's not like I really did. You caught me before I even had a chance."

"It doesn't matter."

"I understand you are angry, and I understand that Freyr feels he needs to punish me for my act. But please, you don't need to tie me. I'll remain in this room and do as both of you ask. I swear it. Just don't tie me up." The thought of being confined like an animal scared me more than what impending doom was to come from Freyr's hand.

Steen took a moment to contemplate my words, and then took hold of the fur on my shoulders, at the same time signaling for me to remove my boots, which I did quickly. "Fine," he said. "But if you try running again, you will have more than just my brother to answer to. I don't like having my kindness taken advantage of. You may not think I'm a smart man but—"

"I would never believe you not to be smart," I interrupted. "Not at all."

Steen walked toward the door with the fur and the boots in his hand. "Just don't push me." He looked over his shoulder. "Things would be so much easier for you, Snow, if you would just stop trying to run. We are huntsmen. We will always hunt you down."

SEVEN

Freyr took two large steps into the room and stood before me. He looked exactly like Steen except he appeared cold...angrier. Dark hair, dark eyes, and dark mood. Freyr didn't have to say a single word to make me understand that he was not a man to be messed with. Power, mystery, and dominance pulsated from his body at the same rhythm as my heartbeat. His firm jaw that clenched while he examined me from head to toe pulled my attention away from his hypnotizing glare. Twin brother with Steen, yet this man before me looked completely different in so many ways.

"Why aren't you tied?" he asked.

"I...uh...Steen said if I was good, I didn't have to be tied. I swear I won't try to escape again."

He remained silent, stony, and cold.

Swallowing back the large lump in the back of my throat, I said, "I need to relieve myself." Maybe it was my body's way of trying to buy time, but I desperately needed to go.

He silently nodded and spun on his heels and walked out the door. Once past the threshold, he looked over his shoulder at where I still stood frozen. "Follow me." His deep voice was firm, direct and sounded so opposite of the way Steen spoke.

I willed my body to follow the man, even though warning bells were going off that this man was not to be trusted. But again, my bladder didn't give me much of a choice.

Leading me outside, to the gathering of large shrubs. I followed him into the area and then turned expecting him to exit and leave me alone. When he remained in place, I asked, "Can you leave?"

"No," was his simple reply. His eyes scanned the area as if he were on guard and my life was in possible danger.

The idea of relieving myself in front of this man infuriated me. "I don't need you to watch over me. I told you that I wouldn't try to escape again."

"Go."

"No," I declared. "I'm not going to go in front of you."

His expression hadn't changed since the moment he'd come for me, but I could see his eyes darken at my refusal.

"Go now." This time his voice stabbed into my soul. I was not going to win this battle, but I still was not going to go in front of him.

"All I ask is that you leave the area a little. I would like some privacy. Please."

"Either go now, or I'll take you back to the house. You can sit in your own filth for all I care. I don't care where you go."

"Fine," I said as I raised my borrowed shirt. "If you don't care where I go," I added as I squatted right in front of him, "I'll go right here, thank you very much." I emptied my bladder right in front of the huntsman, staring directly into his eyes as I allowed every ounce of liquid to release from my body.

Freyr remained emotionless. He didn't say a single word or do a thing. His lack of anger was far worse than any wrath he could inflict. My knees wobbled as I remained in my squat, and I just hoped I wouldn't fall. He scared me. There was no doubt about that, and yet here I was. The fool pissing on the ground mere inches from my captor's boots.

He didn't move. He didn't speak. If I didn't know better, I would say he wasn't even breathing. My action had no effect on him, and I instantly regretted it. My childish tantrum gave him the power. I was now the woman squatting in front of a man with my own waste dripping out of me. Humiliation for me, honor for him. Without doing a single thing, Freyr won this battle, but I had handed it to him.

As I stood and adjusted my shirt, Freyr raised one eyebrow and asked nonchalantly, "Are you done?"

Clenching my teeth, I straightened my shoulders and tried to muster as much dignity as I could as I glided past him, back to the house. I could hear his footsteps behind me, and could almost feel his smugness burning against the back of my head.

I didn't know why I was afraid of the man. He wouldn't kill me or risk upsetting the other huntsmen who all wanted to share me. I was worth a high price to each and every one of them for physical companionship alone. But there was something that terrified me about him. He seemed scarier than some of the other huntsmen.

Freyr reached for my upper arm and took hold. It didn't hurt, but his grasp was tight. He led me into his room and forced me to sit on the edge of the bed by pushing me down. He knelt and reached beneath the bed, pulling a long rope from underneath. He tied one end of the rope around the wooden leg of the bed with several tight knots.

"You don't need to tie me. I told you that I learned that there is no point in running. It won't happen again, I assure you," I said as panic began to set in. "I have no intention of trying to escape."

He didn't reply but instead grabbed me by the back of the neck, pulled my head into him, and looped the rope securely around my neck. It was tight enough that when I swallowed, I could feel my flesh connect with the cool restraint.

Tugging on the rope to make sure it was secure, Freyr said, "You will discover soon enough that my brother and I have very different rules. You will remain tied until I say otherwise."

I reached for the rope and tried to pull it away from the front of my neck to no avail. "Please. It makes it hard to breathe."

"Yes." He stood up, not caring in the slightest.

"Please." I took a deep breath, feeling the walls close in. "I can't breathe. This is making me—"

"Enough," he interrupted. Without saying another word, he exited, leaving me grasping at the rope around my neck, struggling for air.

My heart beat so hard against my chest, that I was positive I would die from the hysteria overwhelming me. I couldn't breathe. I couldn't breathe! I did everything I could to pull the rope away, but the more I struggled, the worse it seemed to get. The rough edges were rubbing my skin raw as I pushed and pulled.

I got up and walked to the mirror to see if I could find a way to remove the restraint. Maybe I could loosen the knots. The heavy rope dragging behind me only pulled at the loop around my neck more. There was enough rope that I could maneuver around the entire room, though awkwardly. When I saw my reflection in the mirror, the contrast of the rope to my white skin made my awful situation even more of a reality. Staring back at me was nothing but a prisoner, tied, restrained, captive.

Running over to the door, but not being able to make it to the threshold completely due to the rope, I screamed loudly, "I can't breathe! This rope is too tight. I can't breathe. Do you hear me? Come back!" I yanked at the rope as hard as I could.

No response.

"Please! Freyr! Steen! Anyone! I swear to you that I will be good. I'll be good and never give you any trouble again. Just please remove the rope around my neck. I can't stand it. Please! I beg you."

No response.

My chest constricted and I wheezed with all my might to take in some air. I would suffocate. I would die. I would die right in this room if someone didn't come and help me.

Crumpling down to the ground, I pulled my knees to my chest and allowed the tears to fall. With my fingers between the rope and my neck, I slowly managed to calm myself just enough to know I wasn't going to die like I'd thought only seconds before. But maybe I wanted to. Maybe I wanted to die so I didn't have to endure being with the huntsmen any further. Seven monsters. Seven demons leading me to hell.

I was so lost in my misery that I didn't hear the door to the room open. The large frame of Steen caught the corner of my eye, notifying me that he had heard my plea.

Looking up at him with tears streaming down my face, I begged, “Please, Steen. I can’t survive with something so tight around my neck.” I pulled at the knotted rope to emphasize my appeal.

He knelt down beside me and looked me straight in the eyes. “Look at me and take slow, deep breaths.” He placed his fingertip on my cheek and stroked softly. “Calm down. You are going to be just fine.”

I shook my head. “No, I can’t breathe.”

He moved his fingertip and gently ran it along the rope where it met my neck. He dipped his finger between the knots and flesh and said, “There is plenty of room. It’s all in your head. You can breathe.”

“No,” I wheezed, continuing to cry. “Please. I already told Freyr, and I will tell the others when they return, but I won’t try to flee again. I swear it. I have learned my lesson.”

He removed his hand from the rope and placed it on my head. Slowly he stroked his fingers through my hair, never taking his eyes away from mine. “Shhh…just calm down. Calm down. Once you are calm, you will see that the rope is giving you plenty of room to breathe."

"Why can't you untie me? Please!"

He shook his head. "Freyr tied you up, which means Freyr is the only one who can untie you. We don't undermine each other around here. His choices are his."

"I'll do anything," I gasped, although I did seem to be breathing better as the moments passed. His gentle touch and petting of my hair did seem to ease some of my distress.

"Deep breaths," he cooed as he leaned in and kissed my cheek with the most tender of touches. "Breathe in, breathe out."

I followed his command and did my best to regain control of my body.

"That's a good girl," he praised. "One breath at a time." He kissed my cheek again and then my forehead, continuing to stroke my sweaty hair. "You are going to be just fine."

Would I be? How could I be *just fine* ever again? I had never been just fine—even before the huntsmen captured me. My stepmother had made sure of that.

"Do I deserve to be treated like an animal?" I asked. It appeared that my words did make a difference as he seemed to be bothered by my question when his eyes narrowed, but I also got the sense that there was no use trying to convince Steen to go against his brother. They had rules and some sort of code that clearly none of them would break.

Steen placed his palms on each side of my face and forced me to stare directly into his eyes. "You need to behave. If you continue to disobey and act out, I promise you that this rope around your neck will be minor in comparison to what will happen in the future. Behave. Do you understand me? You have nowhere to go. No one to protect you other than us. You will only be hunted down again and suffer the consequences—but with huntsmen with far less patience than I."

He extended his hand to assist me up now that I was breathing normally again.

Standing, I took a moment to allow the slight dizziness to dissipate. Steen placed his arm around my body to hold me steady while the room swirled around me. It hadn't taken long to return to my old self.

"Are you hungry?" he asked.

I nodded.

He reached down to the rope and began working at the knots with his thick fingers. "I can untie you from the bed so you can follow me into the kitchen, but I won't remove the rope from your neck. That will be Freyr's choice as to when that can happen."

Steen eventually untied the rope, and the removal of the weight helped ease the pressure on the restriction around my neck a little. He then grabbed my arm and led me out of the room. Entering the main room, I saw Freyr sitting at the table. The room was dimly lit, so the red light emitting from the roaring fire was all the more pronounced. When he looked up, he scowled seeing me walking beside Steen.

"What is she doing out of the room? I'm tired of her antics," he said.

"She's hungry," Steen replied as he pulled out a chair and softly forced me to sit down across from Freyr.

"Feed her and then send her back to the room until the others return," Freyr commanded as he stood to leave the room. It was as if the sight of me made the man sick. How was that so? I had done nothing

—well, unless you counted relieving myself in front of him—to warrant such hatred. "I don't want to be held accountable if she tries to escape while the others are away."

Steen quickly did as he instructed and made me up a meal of dried meat and vegetables. Vegetables! I hadn't had a real vegetable in years due to being locked in the castle for so long. My mouth watered as he put the tin plate in front of me. As I ate bite after bite with pure joy, I temporarily forgot that I was nothing but a captive tied and captured. For now, I ate.

EIGHT

Finding a way to lie on the bed comfortably with the rope still so tight against my flesh wasn't easy, but I knew I had to learn how to accept it, or risk having continual panic attacks which couldn't be an option any longer. I needed to be strong. I had to find strength to survive. I had to. Finding my own internal peace would be the only thing to get me through this ordeal. It had been about an hour or so since Steen had escorted me back to the room, and I had no choice but to just wait. Maybe when the others returned, I would be able to convince one of them that I didn't need to be tied like a mangy mutt.

When the door to the room finally opened, sitting up to face whoever entered, my heart stopped when I saw that it was Freyr who marched into the room.

I remembered once when I was really young, my father and I had watched a huge storm brewing from the west. The clouds swirled around and came at us faster than we could take shelter. We had run as fast as we could while the wind howled around us, slapping at our faces. Rain, lightning, hail. A torrential downpour of chaos all around. I remembered that storm clearly.

Yet...it was nothing compared to the storm standing in the room.

"Do not ever try to appeal to my brother's kindness again," he bellowed, stomping straight toward me.

"What? I don't know what you mean," I stammered, feeling the rope tighten as I scurried back toward the headrest of the bed, terrified at the fury I saw in Freyr's eyes. Steen must have tried to change Freyr's mind about keeping me tethered like an animal. He must have tried to plead my case about the rope around my neck after all. Steen strove to be my lionheart. And evidently...he had lost the crusade.

Freyr bolted in my direction and reached out, grabbing a handful of my hair, pulling me mere inches from his face. "Do you think tears will work? Do you think that begging for mercy will make my brother go against me? Against my will? Do you think you can use your womanly ways to seduce my dope of a twin?"

"I'm sorry," I squeaked. The sting from my hair being yanked by the man caused tears to well in my eyes. "I felt as if I couldn't breathe."

He tugged my hair harder, forcing my head to go back so I had to stare into his predator eyes. My throat stretched—so exposed. I wondered if he would bite down and suck my blood like an ancient monster of which tales were told.

I wanted to apologize. I wanted to plead for compassion. I wanted to reach into the depths of his core and pull out even an ounce of humanity. And yet, the beaten down fighter in me still wanted to kill. He'd claimed earlier that he was tired. Well, I was tired. I was exhausted of being the victim. I had no one. No one would save me. I had to save myself. Somehow. Someway. I wanted to decimate. To destroy. To rip his flesh from his bones with my teeth. Beg or kill. Plead or destroy. The soldier that I didn't even realize was locked away inside me won this battle. The soldier in me took full control.

I spat in his face, smiling when I could see the shock caused by my rebellion twinkle in his eye.

“I hate you,” I said. “You are nothing but a beast. A savage. A cruel man. You are far worse than any of the other huntsmen.”

Without wasting another second, Freyr tore my clothing off so fast and furious that I didn’t even have time to comprehend and try to stop the onslaught. Soon, clothes that once concealed my body, became shreds of fabric tossed around by a creature far from a man before me.

I tried to fight him off, even though I knew it was pointless. He was bigger. Stronger. Freyr would win this battle regardless of how hard I struggled.

But that didn’t mean I wouldn’t try.

“Don’t you touch me!” I screamed as I tried to scratch out his eyes.

Gripping my hands above my head, he flung me back hard against the bed, only giving me a second to realize I was completely nude at this point.

“I will do more than touch you,” he growled. Gripping both my wrists with one of his beefy hands, he unfastened the rope with his free hand and his teeth as he worked to untie the knot.

"Don't want the rope? Allow me to help you then," he said as he removed the rope and tossed it to the floor.

I took a deep breath and ceased in my struggles. Freedom. Unrestricted air.

Still holding my hands firmly above my head, he reached for his belt buckle and released it from his waist. "Not a fan of the rope? How about a different type of binding?"

His eyes told me what he was going to do even before his actions did. The malice pulsed all around the darkness of his demanding eyes. I knew that very moment that I had no choice but to succumb to his vexation.

I shook my head. "Please," I begged as he wrapped the leather around my neck, pulling it through the clasp.

He tightened the belt even more as he straddled my body. He had released my hands, so I was able to pull at the leather to no avail. The more I struggled, the tighter he pulled.

"Can you breathe now?" he asked with savagery lining his question.

I couldn't speak and could only shake my head as

my ears began to ring. I really couldn't breathe as the leather got tighter and tighter.

"Look at me," he demanded. "Look at me!"

I opened my eyes and stared into his eyes, silently begging for my life. My trachea felt the pressure of the belt, so much so that I couldn't even swallow the saliva building up in my mouth.

"I want you to remember this. Whenever you think something I do, or something I dictate is so awful, I want you to remember that it can always get worse. I bet you are wishing for the rope right about now." He tightened the belt even more, causing blackness to edge around my vision. "If you doubt me, if you disobey me, if you ever question my actions, just know that it will be much worse for you. You may think that being with us huntsmen is the worst thing that can happen to you...but you are so very wrong. Deadly wrong."

Where was Steen? Would he really allow his brother to kill me? If not for the fact that I was another human being, would he not want to save me simply for the other huntsmen?

I bucked my hips in a final attempt to throw Freyr from my body before darkness completely took hold.

Freyr looked over his shoulder and down at my writhing legs and then back into my eyes. Without saying another word, he loosened the belt just enough that I could take in a shallow breath of air. It wasn't enough to fully fill my lungs, but enough to keep me alive. Just when I was hoping that Freyr had finally felt I had been taught my lesson enough and he would remove the belt, he surprised me by getting off my body and flipping me over onto my stomach.

A familiar feeling of fear and forbidden arousal took over as the memory of the other huntsmen taking me took hold of my emotions. Would Freyr do the same? Would he take what wasn't his? Would he force me as the others had done? Would he fuck me and then choke me until I died? Would I be nothing more than a fucked and strangled captive—cold, dead, forgotten?

He loosened the belt a little more, this time allowing me to wheeze and gasp. The burn of my lungs eased with every inhale, and the shadows disappeared from my vision. I could breathe—though uncomfortably.

"So will you ever try to escape again?" he asked as he crashed the palm of his hand against my bare behind. "To leave and face the dangers that are far worse outside these walls?" He continued to spank my buttocks, the loud sound of flesh hitting flesh echoing against the walls of the room.

The humiliation of such an act threatened to take back the little air I had just managed to obtain. The belt was still tight around my neck, but I could no longer focus on the struggle to breathe. The searing swats of his hand on my butt were the only thing my mind could address. Desperation crackled from my core, all the way to the tips of my toes. I couldn't cry out, I couldn't plead, I couldn't demand. I could do nothing but gasp for air against firm leather and allow the assault of the spanking to continue.

And oh how it continued.

Over and over, Freyr rained down slap after slap against the entire surface of my exposed skin. I tried to wiggle away to no avail, and was only rewarded for such an action by a harder spank to my ass. The palm of his hand felt the same as if he were using a solid piece of wood or a tawse. Such strength. Such sting. Such mortifying pain.

Silently I begged him to stop. Hoping somewhere deep inside he could read my mind and know how terribly sorry I was. I should have never tried to escape. I should have never for one second forgotten that the huntsmen are my captors and my life was fully in their hands. I was a prisoner, not a guest. I was here by force, not by choice.

Spank after spank, fire erupted from the depths of my ass and sizzled its way to the surface. Tears fell freely from my eyes and my wheezing grew louder against the choking belt that Freyr still held firmly against my neck.

"Would you like me to remove the belt?" he asked while still continuing to spank with fury.

I nodded my head, as it was the only thing I could do.

"Very well. But I am not done with it yet." He paused in the blistering punishment and removed it from my neck. The rush of air that entered my body the moment the pressure released made my head spin with the intensity of oxygen my body so desperately hungered for.

I remained on my belly, absolutely still. I didn't want to give him any reason to continue on and just prayed that he viewed my lack of movement as complete defeat. He was the victor in this battle. I was merely a fallen soldier hanging on by a thread. My prayers were not answered, however, when I felt the lash of leather crack against my already punished flesh.

I screamed out in pain, but more out of shock than agony. "No," I rasped, barely having a voice.

"Yes."

Freyr whipped me with the belt again, and although I wanted to turn around and fight him for doing so, I knew I had no choice but to lie there and take it. I reached for the pillow with both of my hands and squeezed tight as the next blow came down harder than the one before.

"Will you risk your life with another escape attempt?" he asked as he licked me with the harsh sting of leather again.

"No," I answered between clenched teeth.

"No what?" he asked as he continued whipping me.

"No, sir!" I cried. "I will never leave any of you huntsmen."

He cracked the belt against me once more, this time to the spot where my ass met my thighs. "When the others ask if you've learned your lesson, what will you say?"

"That I have learned and paid severely. That I will

never try anything as foolish as leaving," I said as I struggled for air. Between a still sore throat, and the belt lashing, I could barely squeak the words out.

"Good girl," he said as he tossed the belt to the side of the bed. He replaced the belt with the palm of his hand and began caressing my flesh that burned at the gentlest of touches.

I hissed in response.

"Remember this punishment. Your survival will depend on you understanding that you are to allow us to keep you safe. Safe in the hands of me and the others."

I nodded between ragged breaths.

"Never question. Never disobey. Never for one second act out like you did before." He dipped his finger between the juncture of my thighs and collected the juices of my heated sex on his fingertips and brought them to my nose. "Do you smell your arousal?" He raised them to my eyes. "Do you see how wet you are?" He brought his fingers to my mouth and pressed them past my lips. "Do you taste it?"

He forcibly swirled his fingers along my tongue, giving me no choice but to suck his fingers into my mouth, tasting my own musky essence. I had never been this close to my own arousal, let alone known what it smelled like, looked like, or tasted like. I stared into his eyes and licked his fingers clean.

"You like discipline, you like pain."

I shook my head with his fingers still invading my mouth. "No," I mumbled against his fingers.

"Yes," he argued with a slight smile. "Your body betrays you."

How could this be? I hated him. I hated everything about what he did to me and how he treated me... and yet, I wanted his finger to return to my pussy and rub my clit. I wanted his touch. I wanted it more than anything. I hungered. I craved. I needed. My bottom burned, my neck throbbed, but my soul burned for more. I wanted it again. Choke me, beat me, and please, oh please, fuck me.

The devil had truly possessed my body, but no holy water would be able to purge me clean.

Pulling his fingers away from my mouth, Freyr put his face right up to mine. So close that I could feel his breath against my lips. "I will not tolerate. I will not forgive. Where my brother may care, I do not. My brother may be nice; I am anything but. My brother possesses everything that I do not. Remember that."

He pressed his mouth to mine in what I thought would be a kiss, but instead, he pulled my bottom lip in between his teeth and bit hard.

"Do not make me teach you another lesson. I will not hesitate to keep you safe, no matter what it takes to assure that I do," he warned.

NINE

"Are you ready for the last part of your lesson on what happens when you anger a huntsman?"

I nodded. "Yes, teach me," I begged. I wanted pleasure to join the pain which coursed through my body, but more than anything else, I wanted to feel Freyr's cock buried deep within me.

Again, the devil screaming inside of me was so very loud.

Demanding to be heard.

No chance for redemption.

Nothing but sinful lust and damning hunger.

Something had been awoken inside of me via the

pain of the punishment by Freyr's hand. My needs, my desire, my lust all bubbled to the surface, begging for satisfaction.

Freyr glared into my hunger-filled eyes and softly began to speak. "I will have you tonight, Snow. I will take you and make you mine. Completely. And not just me…I will share you with my brother as well."

Both.

Yes. Yes…

I turned my head at the heavy sound of Steen's boots entering the room.

Both brothers.

At once.

Yes, the devil hollered inside of me like never before.

I could feel the lust-induced power begin to take over. His voice echoed, his face blurred. Warm light emanated from his body, and a heat burned between our connecting flesh. My eyes rolled back in my head for a moment while the spell took over my entire being.

Steen turned me onto my back, careful not to cause

any more pain to my punished behind. I could feel his light touch along the surface of my skin.

So much softer than his brother's harsh hand.

Closing my eyes, I focused on the sensations sizzling through me—to the sense of touch alone. The cloak of darkness my eyelids provided heightened every stroke and every glide of their warm touches. The sound of their own clothes being removed, tortured me with the need to see the brothers nude before me.

I moaned in anticipation, knowing what I was doing—or having done to me—was wrong, but I couldn't resist the need to have this. To take...to give... to them both at the same time.

One of the brothers placed a trail of soft kisses along my stomach. I wanted to open my eyes and see who, but part of me was afraid. Afraid to see two men hovering above me. If I kept my eyes closed, it would make this all seem like a dream rather than reality. Reality made it all the more dirty and wrong, but a dream was safe.

The mystery brother's hands moved along the soft mounds of my breasts, gently massaging my fiery skin. Maybe it was both of them—each caressing a breast. A mouth lowered to one of my hardened nipples and a tongue began to trace along the tip. I moaned as the inferno slowly eased from my body. The tongue continued to lick as a hand caressed my throbbing mound. Two fingers trailed down the wet folds before finding my welcoming entrance. Fingers pressed inside, causing a gasp to escape my lips.

I still kept my eyes closed as I tried to concentrate on the sensual feeling of fingers moving in a rhythmic motion inside my quivering pussy while my breast was sucked at the same time—all by two different men. I moaned in delicious agony, but slowly the moans became ones of pleasure.

The fingers worked in and out of my cunny while a mouth nipped at my breast. When I moaned even louder, the mouth moved to my neck, kiss by kiss, lick by lick.

Sucking at my earlobe, Freyr whispered, “Do you want to feel our cocks buried deep inside of you? Do you want to feel the orgasm we give you course through every muscle of your body? Taking away the pain I caused you with your punishment?”

I tried to reply but was unable to speak. I could only moan and thrust my hips against fingers which were still deep within my sex.

A mouth lowered down my torso until he pressed his lips to my awaiting clit, while another mouth growled against my neck, nipping at my ear.

Taking my bud within his lips, he sucked every ounce of residual pain from my body. I finally opened my eyes and looked down to find Freyr staring up at me from between my legs. Steen was caressing my breasts while nibbling and sucking on my neck and ear.

Freyr sucked on my sensitive nub some more, causing me to arch my back in need. He moved his fingers in and out of my hole while sensually licking circles around my sensitive flesh. He added a third finger to join the others, stretching me to the fullest.

My impending orgasm built. A wave of ecstasy worked its way through my body, getting closer to the crash.

"Your taste, your smell...I, I had no idea," Freyr mumbled between sucks of my weeping cunt.

I began to shake, losing my mind to the delirium of what this man and his brother were doing to my body. "Yes! Yes! Yes!" I screamed as the orgasm rocked every inch of my soul.

Freyr softly kissed his way back up to my neck,

savoring every part of my body along the way. His breath was hot against the opposite ear from the one Steen was sucking on, as he whispered, "Now it's my brother's turn to make you scream. He's going to press inside of you. You are going to squeeze that pussy of yours around his cock."

Steen repositioned his body and rubbed his hardness against the wet lips of my pussy causing electricity to shoot through my body. He continued to rub sensually up and down, taking pause to circle the tip of his cock along my throbbing clit still wet from his brother's tongue. Every touch, every movement brought on a wave of ecstasy that lit my body ablaze.

"Oh! Please, please! I need to feel you pressed deep within me. Please," I begged between moans. Any illusion of decency had been discarded the minute I'd crossed the threshold of the huntsmen's house. I was theirs to do with as they chose...and Lord help me, that was exactly what I wanted them to do.

Steen positioned the tip of his penis at my opening and slowly massaged the outer edges. Each teasing movement drove me closer to the impending orgasm waiting to escape my body.

"Come for me first. I want to hear you scream as

you orgasm," he commanded. "I want you to come before I take you completely."

Simply hearing the seductive order from one of my captors was all I needed to allow the release. The smoothness of his cock up against my soft folds only added to the wave after wave of pleasure exploding from my body. I thrust my hips hard against Steen's, straining desperately to force his cock inside me. I would have done anything at that moment to just feel him deep within my core.

Freyr's mouth closed on my neck, teeth grazing my skin as he sucked.

"I'm not handing you off to one of the other huntsmen without a fresh load of my come in that sweet, little pussy of yours." Steen's gravelly tone and the vulgar words caused a catch in my belly. "I want everyone, including you, to smell who you belong to."

Freyr chuckled as he lowered his mouth to my nipple. "You can be a sick bastard, brother."

Steen pressed a hand onto the flat of my stomach as my hips thrust up in silent need, like my sex was an offering, not just for him but for the both of them.

The fat head of Steen's cock entered me without

preamble, thrusting into my core. I gasped in surprised discomfort, focusing on accepting his girth. His big palms held my hips still until my enflamed muscles accepted his thick presence. Then he thrust again, as his eyes locked with mine.

Freyr pressed his lips to mine as Steen pushed even deeper with each movement, grinding his hips against me, until I felt stretched. Full.

"Do you like my brother's cock in that pussy of yours?" Freyr asked when he broke away from the kiss. His voice in my ear was a gritty caress, a velvet growl, as his hands moved over my breasts.

"Yes." I did. My whole body came alive under the power of his words and body.

Steen ground in deeper as Freyr nipped at my breasts hard enough so my chest rose off the bed in delightful agony. "Do you want us both? Tell me." Freyr's voice held a devil's smile, but there was a question there, like he wanted to be sure I liked his aggression, and that I truly was giving myself to him and his twin.

I did. I had never had a need so strong before. Their energy beckoned as if I could hear their pulse beneath their flesh. A drumbeat demanding I march along. I couldn't think, just arched my back and pressed my hips upwards, seeking more of Steen, wanting to pull him deeper into my core.

"Do you want me to fuck you too? Do you want me in your ass while Steen fucks you until you scream?" His voice was insistent; his breath ran along the sensitive hairs on my neck as he spoke. Steen never letting up in his assault had my mind spinning and my body humming along to the rhythm of his fucking.

"Yes," I moaned.

"Tell me," his teeth closed around the sensitive skin of my earlobe. "Tell me you want my cock. You'll like it when I fuck you in the ass with it. Tell me you want my come inside of you."

I was panting now, my pussy leaking wetness around Steen's dick.

"Tell me. Tell my brother. Tell us both that you want double penetration. You want it bad."

"Yes, I...I want it. I want you both. Now." My stomach convulsed again at his low hum of satisfaction. I gasped, reveling in the spikes of pleasure that shot straight to the sensitive nub between my thighs as the filthy words left my mouth and the impure thoughts coated my mind.

Steen let out a long satisfied groan at my words and thrust even deeper, spreading me wide.

They brought something out of me that I'd never known was there. They'd shown me the salacious, raw woman inside who knew what she wanted, and liked it.

"Say it again." Freyr's voice was a growl.

I answered with a ferocious growl of my own. "I want you both." I looked into Freyr's dark, lust-filled eyes. I arched up, clenching my internal muscles around Steen's cock, waiting for the brothers to give me what I so desperately needed.

Steen roared as I clamped down on him like a vise, and then pulled out of me roughly. He laid on his back and positioned me to straddle his body, thrusting his cock in me without even seconds passing to allow me to miss the fullness of his possession. Freyr mounted the bed and pulled back my hips to get in position for him to take me at the same time. I closed my eyes and rode up and down Steen's shaft as I felt Freyr put the tip of his cock against my anus.

"This will hurt," Freyr warned.

"Yes," I panted. God I wanted it to hurt. I wanted to feel the pain.

"No," Steen said, abruptly stopping. "Not her ass. You know that ass of hers belongs to Dagr. He made that clear to all of us, brother."

My heart stopped. Dagr claimed his intent to possess my ass first? This was decided beforehand?

Freyr grunted. "True." He took hold of me with Steen's assistance and flipped me back onto my back. "Well then, I shall feel these sweet lips around my prick."

Steen resumed his position surging forward, holding me immobile so I could adjust to the size of his dick stretching me fully once again while Freyr pushed his hard cock past my lips and deep into my mouth.

I wanted to scream, to moan, to beg for them to stop, but at the same time, I wanted to beg for them to begin. Wave after wave of conflicting emotions and feelings washed over me. Wrong versus right. Pain versus pleasure. Submission versus resistance.

Freyr eased his thickness to the back of my throat, while Steen began thrusting slowly, setting a tempo for the both of them. In and out, back and forth, the two of them fluidly controlled my body. The pressure, the fullness, the dual possession—I had no choice but to succumb fully to their control.

I released everything to them and truly became a slave to their mastery.

They moved rough and fast, pumping furiously in my cunny and mouth until I felt the hot jets of both their climaxes deep within and heavy on my tongue, and a screaming release tore through me, leaving me shaking and gasping for air. My quivering walls milked Steen dry while I swallowed every last drop of cum from his twin. They both regained their composure as a warm heat flowed through my veins.

I couldn't speak, not that I would know what to say if I could. The smell of sex mixed with the thick silence of the room. Even though the three of us were all physically joined as one, we were distant and deep within our own selves. Pleasured, replete, satiated, and yet...there seemed to be a sense of wonder cast over our intertwined bodies. As if we were all questioning how what had started out as nothing more than an animalistic act seemed to affect us all in a way none of us could explain.

TEN

"Sit down and eat your toast and jam like a good girl," said Steen as he handed me a plate with a thick slice of warm bread slathered with butter and boysenberry preserves.

Dutifully nodding yes, I curled my legs up beneath me and snuggled further into the quilt wrapped warmly around my body. It was now becoming my habit to grab the quilt off of whoever's bed I arose from and drag it downstairs to sit before the fire in the morning. It was out of practicality, because I was usually left with no clothes after one of the huntsmen had finished with me. Yes, practicality. It had nothing to do with me wanting to surround myself in their scent or with me associating the warmth of the blanket with the warmth of their arms as they held me in bed as we slept. No, not at all. And it most definitely had nothing to do with me prolonging the memory of what had just occurred. Absolutely not! That would be absurd. Why would I want to preserve memories of pain and fear? Because they weren't just memories of pain and fear, a little voice in my head nagged. They were also memories of intense passion, of feeding off their energy till my core buzzed with it...of finally feeling like I was living! Yes, life in all its messy glory.

No longer driven numb by the cold isolation of my former existence, my life now hummed with every spectrum of emotion...fear, confusion, anger, passion...maybe even love.

These boorish men with their forceful needs were also protective and almost kind in a primitive, dominant sort of way. They showed their kindness in a raw, straightforward manner, like making sure I was eating enough or was warm enough, not with words but with deeds.

As I sat on the cushioned bench, idly staring into the dancing flames, I realized with a start that I was enjoying the attention from these seven men, even enjoying their touch...and if I were completely honest with myself, their punishments. It reminded me of a child who misbehaves just to get attention because after spending so many years being ignored, it was exhilarating to know your every move, your every word, your every deed... and misdeed...was being noticed by someone...that someone cared enough to notice...and react.

I was so lost in my thoughts I almost didn't notice when Odin sat on the bench next to mine and placed a package wrapped in brown paper on the seat beside me.

"What is this?"

Clearing his throat, he gruffly said, "It's just something we picked up for you in town."

Staring at him, I could almost imagine there was a slight blush to his cheek. Pulling on the string, I slowly opened the package, wanting to savor every moment. I had not received a gift from someone since my father died all those years ago. Placing the string aside, I opened the folds of the crisp brown paper to reveal a folded piece of fabric in a bright, beautiful yellow. It looked like the plumage of a bird with its cheerful color. Touching the cloth almost reverently, I reveled in the soft, silky feel. Lifting the fabric up, I realized it was a skirt and underneath was a linen blouse, and a vest in deep blue with shiny, polished buttons. Beneath the clothing was a pair of black slippers.

"Oh, Odin! They are lovely!" I exclaimed as I jumped up and impulsively placed a kiss on his cheek.

Hiding a smile, he blushed and bashfully lowered his head. "It's nothing. Just a bit of finery we thought you might like, lass."

"Besides, we are all running out of shirts for you to ruin," chimed in an amused Magni.

"It is not *I* who tears them off my body!" I responded indignantly.

My spirited response got a rousing laugh from all the men.

"Try them on. Let's see if they fit," piped in Jerrik.

Feeling a little shy from all the attention, I awkwardly tried to hold the quilt around my shoulders and gather up the garments to take them upstairs so I could change.

"Where are you going?" asked Dagr.

"To put on my new clothes."

"You can stay right here before the fire and do that."

"Here?"

"Here," they all responded in unison.

It was not the first time they had made me bare myself to their eyes, but this time it felt...different. Before, I'd felt humiliated and degraded, but now I had this strange sense of empowerment. This surge of excitement from being the center of attention to so many brawny men. I was still nervous and shy but in an intense, sensual way.

Slowly, I let the blanket fall from my naked shoulders.

From their appreciative gazes, I knew they were pleased both with my obedience and with my body. Before, it had been just my body, nothing special, but since becoming the captive of the huntsmen, I had developed a whole new awareness of myself. Of the heavy feel of my breasts when they touched me. How my stomach clenched in fear and anticipation. How rough their hands felt on my soft skin when they stroked my thigh or back. Of the tingling sensation between my legs when they looked at me as they were now.

So far, I had only experienced them one at a time with the exception of my punishment with Freyr and Steen. What would it be like to have that intense attention from all of them at the same time, my wicked mind wondered unbidden? Confused and shocked by the nature of my thoughts, I concentrated on quickly donning the new clothing.

I was pleased and proud when they clapped and whistled their appreciation for how I looked. They made me twirl and dance about so they could all get a look at my new attire. A few of them even took me into their arms and showed me the steps of a country jig.

Yes, I was definitely enjoying this strange new existence of mine.

ELEVEN

"No!" I shouted with all my might. "I may be your prisoner but I am still a princess, not a scullery maid."

"Lass, you will do as you are told. We all pull our weight here. Even you," scolded Tore.

The atmosphere in the cabin had taken on a tense, dangerous feel. Tore was correct. Everyone did chores around the cabin, but I didn't feel that should also include me. I might have been adapting to my new situation, but that didn't mean I wasn't still forced into it. In my mind, I was already doing my part by obeying their wicked demands in bed. Did I have to scrape and clean like a servant as well?

Crossing my arms over my chest, I became adamant. No matter what the punishment, I refused to be forced onto my knees to scrub the floor. It was one indignity too far in my estimation. Especially since it was likely to ruin my pretty new skirt.

"Men. Go without me. It is past time Snow received a punishment from me," said Dagr as he lowered his gear to the floor and began to slowly unbutton the thick leather vest he always wore.

Lowering my arms, I looked about me. Out of all the men, I was most afraid of Dagr. With his dark eyes and lowered brow, it seemed as if a turbulent mood always simmered just below the calm surface of his regard.

Running over to Steen, the gentlest of the men, I grabbed his arm. "Please, don't leave me with him."

Steen shook his head giving me a sympathetic look. "You brought this on yourself, little one." He loosened my grip and followed the other men out the door.

The cabin descended into silence.

Dagr took a step forward.

Stretching my arm out in front of me, I cried out, "Stop! Don't you come any closer!"

His only response was a deep chuckle as he began to roll up the linen cuffs of his sleeves.

I had only one choice...run.

Bolting for the stairs, my foot barely touched the smooth wood of the first step before a strong arm wrapped around my waist and snatched me up high. Bucking my hips as I kicked out, I called him every vile curse I had recently learned from overhearing the men's conversations.

His only response was that infuriating chuckle.

Letting out a howl of frustration, I clawed at his arm around my waist to no avail. He lifted me as if my weight was of no consequence and carried me to his bedroom.

The moment my feet touched the soft wool rug, I ran to the farthest corner. I had yet to be alone with Dagr and had never seen his inner sanctuary. Furtively looking about me, I was horrified to see every manner of wild beast staring back at me from the walls.

Vacant glassy eyes. Bared teeth. Vicious horns.

The entire chamber was an homage to Dagr's dominance over these animals. A display of his superior strength and cunning. His trophies on display. I didn't stand a chance.

"Please. Please. I'm sorry. I didn't mean it. I'll scrub the floors. Please!"

I watched in horror as he pulled his shirt over his head. His massive chest was only lightly dusted with coal black hair and covered in thick muscle, earned from hard labor. I could see the faint pink scars from old wounds. Small circular starbursts from wounds of the past. Long jagged lines from knives.

My inner thighs clenched. Despite my fear, I could feel a primal response to his display of brute, almost violent, strength. A deep feminine yearning. An ancient need to be claimed and protected by the fiercest and strongest of the clan.

I'd survived Freyr and Steen's intense punishment.

I was not sure I would survive Dagr's.

I tried to appease him again. "Please let me just scrub the floor. I will even wash all the clothes without the slightest complaint just please...*please*...don't punish me."

Dagr reached for the heavy buckle of his thick, leather belt.

As he loosened the strap, I shrank further back into the darkened corner less afraid of the beasts on the wall than I was of the beast in front of me.

"Snow, there are rules. You may have not chosen this new life of yours...but it is your life now. Disobedience leads to disorder, and with disorder comes danger and death. Everyone and everything in this world has a place and purpose. You need to learn yours. But by god, by the end of this night, you will know both."

Unwrapping his belt, he flipped the long leather strap over a large tangle of horns which were suspended from the high ceiling.

I had not noticed it at first and now I did not know how I could have missed it. It spanned almost the length of my body. A macabre chandelier of antlers, horns and bone.

I watched in stunned confusion as he wrapped his belt around the large bone which ran the length and then buckled it to make a wide loop. Walking to a worn leather trunk at the end of the bed, he pulled free more leather straps and thick rawhide ropes.

Without even glancing my way, he commanded, "Take off your clothes, Snow."

Wrapping my arms around my middle, I hesitated.

"You just got those pretty garments. It would be a shame if I was forced to tear them off you."

His quietly uttered threat might as well have been a bellow for its effectiveness. Without another moment's hesitation, my shaking fingers flew to the buttons of my blue vest. They had only given me a shirt, skirt and a vest...no undergarments. My breasts felt heavy as the constraining fabric of the vest loosened. Trying to bide my time, I carefully folded it and placed it to the side. Wanting to keep the protective, albeit flimsy, covering of the linen shirt for as long as possible, I reached back to unbutton the skirt. Reluctantly, I let it fall to my slippered feet.

All the while, I watched him weave several rawhide ropes and another leather strap around the various antlers and horns.

Bending over, I removed my new slippers. I hesitated.

"All of your clothes, Snow. I want you completely bare," he ordered, again without even looking my way, as if he had a sixth sense for my movements.

Catching on the neckline of the shirt, my long black curls flipped up, then bounced down around my shoulders, not quite reaching my nipples as I pulled the fabric over my head.

Nervously, I shifted from foot to foot as a shiver ran down my spine despite the warm room. Under my lashes, I watched him remove his trousers. Heavy, muscled thighs, covered with more dark hair first met my gaze. Then, I caught sight of his cock, jutting proudly from between his legs. Swallowing in fear, I closed my eyes to block out the vision of the thick, long shaft. After a moment, I opened them again, not wanting to be caught unaware.

Walking over to the wall, Dagr unfurled the rope from around a wooden lever. The antler chandelier slowly lowered till it was several feet from the ground. He secured the rope around the lever and turned to me.

His dark eyes seemed to glow in the candlelight. His anticipation was palpable from the tense set of his shoulders to his fisted hands, to the firm set of his jaw. He radiated barely restrained arousal.

I didn't dare look...*there.*

I opened my mouth to speak...to plead...to beg... but no sound came out. Just a pitiful squeak.

Placing his finger under my chin, he raised my head to his gaze. I could feel him taking my measure. Unconsciously, I licked my lips. He bared his teeth and let out a low growl. Slipping his hand behind my neck, he propelled me across the room. Placing his warm hands around my waist, he lifted and placed me on the leather loop created with his belt. The sharp edges of the leather cut into the lush flesh of my bottom as I tried to adjust my awkward position.

"Don't move."

"But...what—"

"Don't move."

Dagr then grabbed my left ankle and lifted it high, securing it inside a rawhide loop. I reached up to grab onto a pair of antlers just above my head as I strained to keep upright. He grabbed my other ankle and did the same. My legs were now outstretched on either side of his narrow hips. I blushed to see his gaze wander to my open and exposed cunny. The belt cut painfully into my skin now that my full weight was seated on the narrow strip of leather. I watched as Dagr circled behind me. I tried to turn my head to see what he would do next, but another darkly uttered reminder to stay still had me obediently facing forward.

His fingers delved into my hair. Sharp pricks of pain erupted across my scalp as he cruelly pulled on my long locks, forcing my head and torso back.

I cried out as my hands lost their grip on the smooth surface of the horns, and I fell backward. My body swung on my precarious perch as his strong hands used his grip on my hair to force me into a prone position.

"Lift your bottom and shift forward. Don't stop till you feel the leather against your lower back."

Anxious and uncertain, I could only obey.

With his hand supporting my head, I shifted forward. I could then feel him place another leather strap under my neck. Completely suspended by the straps, I floated a few feet below a tangled web of horns and antlers...a trophy among trophies.

Dagr placed himself between my legs. My eyes widened as in my increasing agitated state, it looked as if he himself had turned into a beast. The horns from the chandelier appeared to crown his disarrayed locks and fierce brow.

"Please, I don't like this. I'm scared."

"Lass, you don't know what fear is *yet*."

Unable to take it a moment longer, I tried to sit up but my movements were ungainly given my precarious perch. In this unstable seat, I watched as Dagr released the rope holding the chandelier. I could not suppress a cry of shock as the chandelier pitched downward, jarring me as it very nearly hit the floor before being hoisted higher. Straining my neck to the side, I watched in horror as the ground receded.

Higher and higher.

Finally, my ascent stopped. Dagr approached. My prone body was just about in line with his shoulders. At first, I tried to twist and turn but quickly learned the slightest movement caused my leather sling to sway and pitch to an alarming degree.

My fear and panic were replaced by alarm when I felt Dagr's warm hand on my bottom. It hung at a humiliating angle, jutting out beneath me.

"Such a beautiful trophy," murmured Dagr. "That is what you are, Snow. A hunting trophy to me."

Gripping the horns above my head, I tried to lift my hips to move away from his touch.

There was the sickening sound of flesh hitting

flesh before a hot burst of pain radiated across my buttocks.

"Move away from me again and I will get a belt and tan your hide," he growled.

I bit my lip to keep from sobbing. Never in my life had I felt more vulnerable or more at the mercy of another person's whim.

His hands closed over the lower swell of my bottom cheeks, prying them open.

"Look at that untouched little hole."

Remembering back to the night they stole me away and the other huntsmen's comments about Dagr, I could no longer contain my sobs.

"I beg you! Don't! I can't! Please!"

"You can, and you will, Snow."

"No! No! Please!"

I started to struggle. The antler chandelier swayed and rocked with my movements. It was all futile. I was trussed and tied as if I truly were the hunting prize Dagr claimed.

His strong hands pinched my bottom cheeks as he forced them open. Then I felt the whisper of a breath against my cunny, then my hidden hole. I moaned as the light hint of breath sent a shiver of awareness coursing through my body.

"You are so sensitive you shudder at my very breath."

"No," I groaned in protest.

I then felt his lips on my cunny. The tip of his tongue laved at the folds of my sex, seeking entrance. I moaned as he shifted his hands to place his thumbs between my legs and used them to open me...expose me...to his touch...his tongue. He laved again, this time brushing my sensitive nub. With the tip of his tongue, he circled and teased my center, sending wave after wave of heated, unwanted sensations through me. Swirling. Tasting. Pressing then receding only to press again. Each flick of his tongue a ruthless reminder of his power over me. My hips bucked. The leather belt dug into my lower back with the movement, surely marking me, but I didn't care.

My toes curled as he continued to flick his tongue over my nub.

"Oh god! Oh god! You have to stop. Please! I can't," I begged to no avail.

The pressure began to build. I was floating free, yet restrained. I felt dizzy and numb, while at the same time sensitive and extraordinarily aware of every moment, every sigh, every single feeling.

The pressure continued to escalate. My release was upon me.

Then…then…

His tongue moved down. Applying pressure to the tip, he lapped at the puckered skin of my hidden entrance.

“No! Stop! Don’t!” I cried out.

He slowly pushed the tip in and out of my entrance. It was wrong. It was depraved.

Still he tortured me.

Swirling, laving, licking.

Knowing with each flick of his tongue, my mortification increased. How? How could I possibly like the feel of his tongue, there? It defied reason. And yet…oh god.

“Your bottom hole is sensitive. I believe you would come from my very breath on it,” he growled against my skin.

The vibrations of his deep, dark words sent me over the edge. Losing my grip on the horns above me, my arms dangled helplessly to my side as my head tilted all the way back. My mouth opened on a deep-throated moan as my inner thighs twitched against his jaw.

My release was all encompassing, transcending my fear and humiliation.

"Good girl," he chuckled as I dangled above the floor, replete and panting. "Now it is my turn," he warned as he slowly lowered me down a few feet till I was trussed in my binds right at his hips.

I was too dazed and overwhelmed to embrace the impact of his words. It was not until I felt a cool ointment being spread between my bottom cheeks that I reacted.

"What is that?"

"It is more of Tore's salve. It will help you accept my cock up your ass without tearing."

"No! You cannot mean to do this to me. You will kill me!"

"You will be in pain, but trust me, you won't die."

Squirming within my binds, I tried to lift my hips and contort my body in a desperate effort to resist his touch. It only earned me another stinging spank to my right cheek.

Dagr positioned his brawn between my legs. Looking down my leather trussed body, I watched in abject fascination as he fisted his cock. It was as if he held a wild animal. Thick, swollen and pulsing. It seemed to turn an angrier red the more he handled it.

My breath came in short, frantic gasps. Everything swirled about me. The contorted shapes of the antlers and horns. The smell of our warm skin which held the musky scent of arousal and sweat. The imagined sound of my own pounding heart. The bite of the leather restraints as they stuck to my damp skin, further restricting my movements.

Placing his hands on my upper thighs, he pushed down. My hips slipped lower as the belt moved up higher on my back. My bottom was now obscenely on display as my legs opened wider. I clung to the leather straps to keep from falling.

"I'm slipping."

"You're not."

"Please! I'll fall."

"You won't. Now tell me, where is my cock?"

As he ground out the words, I could feel the tip of his cock against my tight entrance.

"Please! You—"

"Where is my cock?"

The head pushed forward. Instinctively, I clenched down, tightening the puckered entrance, refusing him entry. The salve, warmed from the heat of my body, began to drip down the crease of my bottom, tickling my skin. Placing his hands on my thighs, he pushed again. This time, eased by the heated salve, the head began to crest, pushing through my resistance. I tried to clench harder. Still he pushed. I could feel my body being forced open. There was a burning, stretching sensation, then the head pushed through. The momentary release of pressure was almost satisfying till I felt him thrust forward. His thick shaft was driving deeper into my body.

"It hurts!" I screamed. "Stop!"

"No," came his ruthless, curt reply.

His shaft pushed forward, forcing my body to accept him. I could feel every inch as my muscles strained and clenched.

"Where is my cock?" he asked again.

"In me," I whimpered.

Digging his fingers into my thighs for purchase, he pulled back and then thrust forward.

Screaming, my whole body bucked as the antler chandelier I was trussed to swayed and rocked.

"Where is my cock?" he shouted.

"In my ass. In my ass, oh god," I screamed in return.

He pulled free.

I sobbed with relief, but it was short lived. After waiting the sparest of moments for my body to close in on itself, he thrust forward again, violently forcing my bottom hole to accept every inch of his thick shaft.

I screamed in agony. The burning hot pain pierced me straight through. My stomach twisted and clenched. It felt as though he were severing my insides.

"Take it. Take every inch," he commanded through clenched teeth.

My only response was a pitiful wail as he pummeled my body with his cock.

As his thrusts gained in ferocity, my own body

began to sway in its binds, back and forth, complicit in its own torture as his cock drove deeper and deeper with every swing.

My entire world was centered on his touch and the pain.

“Damn your ass is tight. I can feel you clench and grab at my cock with every thrust.”

“Please, it hurts.”

“This is a punishment. It’s supposed to hurt. I want it to hurt. I want you to feel every painful inch of my cock as I remind you who is in charge of you and your body.”

His hands cupped my bottom as he lifted me up, relieving the pressure of the leather belt against my back and legs. With his steadying grip on my body, his thrusting increased, each powerful shift of his hips hit me like a punch.

I felt bruised and used. My body ached as my stomach cramped from the onslaught.

Still he thrust. Still he pounded into my flesh. Possessing me. Owning me. Dominating me.

A sick primal curl of emotion unfurled deep within me. Despite the pain, the idea of him taking me, claiming me called to some raw, dark corner of my psyche.

Then...he did the unthinkable.

As he thrust, he reached between my legs and stroked my sensitive nub. The confusing mixture of pain and pleasure was too much for my already agitated state.

"You're such a dirty little thing. You like my cock up your ass. You like the pain. Admit it."

I looked between my legs to where he stood. His skin glistened with a sheen of sweat. The shifting glimmer of the candlelight enhanced the edged grooves of muscle and sinew on his body, fixing me with a dark, fierce gaze as he bared his teeth from the exertion. The very epitome of raw, primal power...of man...of a man claiming what was his...by force.

"Yes, damn you! Yes!" I screeched like a harridan as I actually shifted my hips to force my body to sway into his...to force his cock deeper into my ass.

Just as I felt my release crest, he pinched my nub, the spark of pain pushing me over the edge.

I heard his roar of completion as he released his seed deep inside my body...deep inside my ass.

I could only whimper and sigh as he lowered my body to the floor and released me from my leather binds. I could feel his seed trickle out of my now stretched and open hole as he wrapped me in a blanket and carried me downstairs.

TWELVE

Wrapped in my soft cocoon, I pretended to sleep as I could hear the other huntsmen enter the cabin.

Dagr had me on his lap before the fireplace. Insisting I eat, he'd spoon fed me stew like a child till I had drifted off to sleep. The bustling and loud entrance of the other men woke me.

"Quiet. The lass is sleeping."

"Had a rough time of it did she?" said Freyr, a knowing lilt to his words.

Under my lashes, I could see Tore give him a punch on the arm. "You know the rules. We don't discuss each other's time with Snow."

It was comforting to know they didn't discuss my shameful reactions to their touch and punishments amongst one another.

"We have a problem," said Magni. His voice held an unusual serious tone.

"There is talk in the village that Snow is not dead," said Jerrik.

"How is that possible? The queen accepted the boar's heart for Snow's without question," responded Dagr.

Sitting on a bench next to Dagr, Odin explained, "Apparently, us buying the lass' frippery and finery was remarked upon in the village. It's also been noticed that we haven't been spending any time at the pub or perusing other amusements in the last weeks."

"For all her faults, the queen is a smart woman," said Freyr.

Nodding toward Jerrik, Steen said, "Jerrik overheard some of the serving girls talking about how erratic the queen has become as of late. They even overheard the queen cursing the huntsmen and threatening revenge. Talk of finishing the deed herself. It has started the rumor that perhaps the queen was not honest about Snow being killed by marauders."

With my own head still on his shoulder as I pretended to sleep, I could feel Dagr shake his head. "I don't like this, men. We knew our plan to save the lass for ourselves instead of killing her was a risky one, but I think I speak plainly for us all when I say we didn't expect to *feel* for the lass as we do now. I, for one, have no intention of letting her go."

There was a chorus of agreement from the men.

"You know this is insanity. If we were smart, we would give the girl some money and send her as far away as possible," reasoned Tore. "It's the safest option for the lass and for us. It was also what we always intended to do once we had our fill."

I could feel Dagr's hold on my body tense as he instinctively pulled me tighter to him.

There was a long heavy silence.

"Well men, do you think that's what we should do?" asked Dagr gruffly.

My stomach clenched at the thought. The confusing reality was I didn't want to go back to the silence and isolation of being alone. I had grown to love the energy, noise and passion of my new life with the huntsmen. I waited, barely daring to breathe for their answer.

"No," came Magni's decided answer. "The lass is ours and I say we stay and fight for her. The girl deserves a home and life. I'm not going to let some bitter queen take that away from her."

"I'm with Magni. Snow's home is with us where we can protect her. I say she stays," said Freyr.

"And the rest?" asked Dagr.

Desperately I tried to peek from beneath my lashes, but I could not see what they were about, in my heart I hoped they were nodding yes.

"Then so say we all. The lass stays."

I felt Dagr rise. "Jerrik, will you take Snow to your room for the night? Watch over her and keep her occupied while the rest of us plan our defense against the queen."

I was lifted into Jerrik's arms. Still pretending to sleep, I caught a glance of the other huntsmen over Jerrik's shoulder. Their heads bent in serious discussion...planning...all for my protection.

❄

JERRIK CRADLED me in his arms and carried me up the stairs as if I weighed absolutely nothing. His effortless motions as he held me tight offered me a bit of comfort even though absolute panic was setting in.

She was coming after me.

My stepmother was coming, and the huntsmen knew my life was in danger. I could hear it in each one of their voices. Such powerful, domineering, brutes of men, but I could hear the fear for me in the way they spoke. I was supposed to be dead and had been living on borrowed time without even knowing it. The huntsmen—my captors—had been protecting me all along. This cabin was not my prison as I had once believed it to be. Unbeknownst to me, this home of theirs had been my sanctuary, my own protected castle guarded by my seven beasts.

When we reached Jerrik's room, I opened my eyes and looked around, noticing it was similar to all the others I had been in. Though the big difference in this room... this time... was that I had no fear of this man. I did not fear what would happen to me by being alone with him. I did not scan the room looking for an escape route or a possible weapon.

In fact, I had never felt safer as I rested in his arms entering his small and cozy quarters.

Being far more gentle than I thought it possible for any of the huntsmen to be, Jerrik laid me down on his quilt-covered bed with nothing but warmth in his deep brown eyes. He removed the blanket that I had been wrapped in, but didn't seem too focused on my complete nudity at the time. As he pulled the blankets up over me, and he remained standing, it dawned on me that he wasn't planning on joining me in the bed.

I took hold of his forearm. "Don't leave me."

He leaned down and kissed my forehead. "Don't worry. You'll be all right. We are all going to be downstairs talking."

"No, not you. Please," I pleaded like a scared little girl who had just woken from a terrible nightmare.

Except my nightmare was reality. I had a crazed woman with the mission of seeing me killed. There were no sweet, loving dreams in my life. Only dark, evil, deathly nightmares.

"Snow, we aren't going to allow anything to happen to you. We have kept you safe for this long, and we intend to keep it that way."

"Why?" I asked softly, still clinging to his arm. "Why would you keep me safe?"

With a smile, he sat down on the edge of the bed and placed his rough, callused hand on mine. "Because you have managed to accomplish the impossible. You have tamed the wild beasts in this house. We were all nothing but ruthless creatures who only cared for ourselves. But when you came, things changed. I have seen it in each one of my fellow huntsmen. Even the ones who may refuse to admit it. You have captured their hearts far more than we have ever captured you."

"How can that be?"

With a small chuckle, Jerrik bent down and pressed his lips to mine and gave me a soft and gentle kiss. "You have done the impossible just by being who you are. There isn't a man downstairs who wouldn't die for you. I don't have to be down there myself to know that they are all preparing a plan, and acknowledging the fact that your life is worth theirs to save."

"My stepmother is a powerful woman. She has armies."

Jerrik nodded. "We know."

"I don't want any of you to die for me."

He patted my arm again. "That is for us to worry about. Not you. I can see that you are tired, and you need your rest." He stood, breaking free of my grip.

I sat up, feeling a surge of panic attack the heart that he had just warmed with his tender words. "Please, Jerrik. Lie with me until I fall asleep. I don't want to be alone."

He leaned down and softly kissed my forehead once again. I looked up and smiled as our eyes connected. Jerrik didn't pull away, and his lips were so close to mine that I could almost taste his breath... his passion and desire for more.

As if under a spell, I raised my head just enough so that our lips touched in the softest of kisses. Jerrik didn't move back or resist, but quite the opposite. He pressed his lips harder to mine and conquered my mouth with his—fully kissing me as a man would a woman. When his tongue danced with mine, I let out a gasp, breaking the spell we were in.

Jerrik took my hands, linking our fingers together. He lifted my hands, brushed his lips over the back of each one in turn, causing a small tremble to wrack my naked body. He then positioned our bodies on the bed, spooning my curves against his. I pressed my bare bottom against his growing cock that tented his pants.

"I haven't had the chance to be with you, yet, Jerrik. Please, make me yours. Take my body completely." I moaned loudly and without shame as I pressed against him even harder. I wanted him desperately. I craved these soft touches, these warm feelings that blanketed me in security, offering shelter from the raging storm that surrounded me.

He ran his fingertips along the surface of my upturned butt and dipped between the crease, running them from my anus, to my taint, to my weeping hole, to my clit. "Look how wet you are." He pushed a finger past my folds and into my cunny and began pumping it in and out. "Is this your desire for me?"

"Yes," I barely said between my gasps.

He added a second finger to the one already inserted and pumped in and out of me.

Moving lower down my body, Jerrik cupped my hot-skinned mound in his hands, clearly pleased to find me wet with my legs spread wide. I reached for him beneath his clothing, tearing them off him as fast as I could discard the final obstruction between us. He was thick and hard, the massive girth of his cock swollen and leaking. Just for me.

"Let me suck on you," I pleaded. "I want to taste you."

Jerrik granted me my wish as he removed the rest of his clothing and then straddled my neck so his cock rested in front of my face. Moving fast, I sucked him deeply into my mouth, running my tongue along the tip, luxuriating in the heady taste of him. I wanted more.

I raked my nails down his chest and pulled him into my throat until he bottomed out, delightfully gagging me with his size. Still, I tried to take more, until I gagged again, and my mouth salivated. My lips spread wide, he was too big. I'd never get enough of him. His smell and taste were like a poisoned tonic killing the purity I had, once upon a time. The heat of his body, the comfort of his solidity, a balm to an existence that had become fraught, rocky, and confusing.

Jerrik stood at the center of my story, rigid and impregnable. Constant. Reliable.

I moaned around his hard flesh, anxious for the flavor of his release. He groaned when I palmed his sack, squeezing gently.

He thrust against my throat, his hips working, pushing deeper.

"Jerrik." I tried to say his name as he deserved, but it came out muffled. He didn't care, and neither did I.

His fingers dug into my scalp as he pulled my face tighter against his groin, and speech was impossible, so I just hummed around him.

The pre-cum of his desire coated my tongue, thick, heavy, and sweet. I moaned as the serum's aphrodisiac worked through my body, setting nerves tingling. I swallowed him down, sucking until he would have no choice but to release fully into the back of my throat, but he resisted.

"No, I want to fill your cunt with my seed."

Frantically, he lowered himself down and reached for his cock to guide the brutal length of himself between my thighs, pressing past my slick folds, claiming me once again. He raised his hips and slammed back down, pounding into me with everything he had.

One of his hands closed over my breast, fingers strumming my nipple. I groaned as I arched my back, silently begging for more. I wanted him deeper. I wanted to feel his possession so deep that I would truly feel as if we blended as one. I couldn't get enough of him. It was as if my body was starved and it was Jerrik who gave me life.

"Deeper," I moaned, being so bold as to do so.

He groaned out a wordless answer, deep in his throat and my stomach coiled tight at the rasping sound. Flipping us over, he lay on his back and had me straddle him, riding him like some mythical creature. I bobbed up and down as his eyes watched my breasts bounce. I liked having the power to give him pleasure. I could see it in his green eyes. I could feel it coming from his sun-kissed flesh. I pleased him and that very knowledge brought on a wave of euphoria as a tidal wave came crashing down.

I arched my back and screamed out his name as his cock drove deep inside. Over and over again. *Jerrik. Jerrik. Jerrik.*

He grabbed me with a rough hand to the neck, pulling my face down. He sucked at my tongue, swallowing my orgasmic groans. I bit his lip, tasting his blood and bucked my hips, milking the last wave of my release.

I reared up, gasping, reveling in the big cock that slammed deep inside of me with every thrust of his hips. Jerrik looked wild, the thick muscles of his abdomen and chest rippling, his hair curling around his ears.

I dug my fingers into his chest and he groaned again. My thighs burned. I didn't care. None of it mattered. All that mattered was giving this huntsman the pleasure I so desperately wanted to give him.

I leaned back, resting my hands on his corded, muscled thighs so I could get a better angle. His eyes burned into me, dark and probing, hard and hot, as if he saw into my soul. Every time he looked at me, I felt our bond grow stronger and stronger.

The orgasm coiled tight within me again, drawing close.

He slipped a hand down to stroke my clit, and I allowed him to throw me over the edge as he thrust his final release into me with a deep growl. I screamed as a flood of light knocked the wind out of me. Wave after wave of heat coursed through my veins as Jerrik pumped his seed inside of me.

After several breathless moments, Jerrik stood up and pulled on his pants.

"No, please." I still didn't want him to leave me. "Not yet. Not tonight."

"I'll be right back," he said softly with a smile. "Wait right here."

I sat on his bed, hearing the deep voices in heated discussion below. I considered getting dressed in one of Jerrik's shirts and making my way downstairs to join them, but Jerrik had told me to remain in the room, and I really didn't want to test his tender heart. I knew he had the capability of being just as strict and unyielding as the others.

Just as I was getting antsy enough to risk discipline by Jerrik's hand, he walked into the room carrying a pail of water that had been heated by the fire downstairs while I sat on the edge of the bed and waited for him to return. He had kept his tunic off since our intimacy, revealing his tan skin and his muscled arms. With each move, I noticed how lean his body was which surprised me. He wasn't as large in frame as the other huntsmen. I hadn't paid attention before to how handsome he truly was. His brown hair hung in a soft wave around his ears with just a hint of gray at his temples. His distinguished look added to a masculinity that fascinated me. His caring nature made me feel safe and protected.

He soaked a rag in the water and ran it along my

bare thigh. "Is the water too hot?" he asked, worried.

"It's perfect. Simply perfect." I closed my eyes, savoring how the heat removed all the tension in my body. "Thank you."

He moved up my leg with a bar of soap and began lathering it into his palm, his fingers massaging every inch of my legs. Heaven. Pure Heaven. I thought about stopping him and doing it myself, but just couldn't bring myself to do so. It felt so good... so good.

He began washing between my legs, my belly, my breasts, and my arms, dipping the rag into the soapy water with each pass.

"Thank you," I said. "You really don't have to be so kind."

He paused in washing me, holding his hand still in the sudsy water. "You do know we will never allow her or anyone to harm you? Right?"

I nodded, knowing that he meant the words, but still not fully convinced that they all truly had the power to protect me from my demons, and from the ultimate predator—the queen.

He stood up and walked over to grab a shirt of his.

He held it out for me to step into, but turned his head to not watch as I did so. I had to smile at the chivalrous act of affording me privacy. After all, he'd not only fucked me, he'd washed me intimately. Once I had the shirt on, I thanked him.

"Let's get you back in bed before you catch a chill." When he had me tucked in nice and tight, he turned to gather the pail of water.

"Jerrik? Please don't leave. I know you want to join the others, but at least stay with me until I fall asleep." Maybe it was asking too much, but I didn't want to stare at the ceiling for the remainder of the night in worry.

He paused for a moment as if considering the idea. He nodded with a smile and pulled up a nearby wooden chair so it rested beside the bed and sat down. "All right. I'll stay until you sleep. Sweet dreams, Snow. Your nightmares will soon be washed away."

THIRTEEN

The midday sun dipped behind the clouds, chilling the air with its shadow. I sat on a wooden bench in front of the cabin with a fur wrapped tightly around my shoulders. A gentle breeze blew my hair into my face. Blackbirds cawed in the sky—their fragile wings carried them through the air above the trees with ease. The yard was quiet, peaceful, and serene. It reminded me of the palace from my childhood. A life I wasn't sure I would ever live again. I found it odd that, sitting here now was truly the first time I had just sat and taken in my outside surroundings. My life had been in such chaos...but now, things seemed calmer. More at peace. The huntsmen in all their torrential energy had somehow calmed me.

The closing of the door behind my shoulder broke the still energy. "It's time we teach you how to fight," Tore said as he walked in front of me, the other huntsmen close behind.

Dagr pulled a bow from behind his back, his coy smile making me nervous. "Are you ready to learn how to shoot it?"

The hair on my arms stood and my stomach churned with the thought of holding a weapon in my hands, let alone shooting it. Weapons and violence were against everything I once believed in. I was not a fighter or a killer. I'd never had the desire to learn how to be either. But so much had changed, and a deep thick blackness had taken hold of my life and was only getting darker. The war had just begun. The queen was coming, and I knew this in my deepest part of my heart.

“I don't think I have the ability to do this,” I said as I watched Odin and Steen pull out bows of their own. Standing up, I pulled the fur tighter around me as if it were enough to protect me from everything.

"Of course you can, and we'll teach you. Do you see those trees over there?" Freyr asked, pointing north from where we stood. Ten or twenty yards away, two small pines were spread a few feet apart from one another.

“You think I can fire an arrow that far?” I asked.

He ignored my question, took the bow from Tore, and handed it to me. "Everyone should know how to shoot an arrow. Never depend on someone else for your survival. Never."

I glanced at Jerrik who walked up to stand to my left. “You know the queen is coming,” he said. “We want to make sure you can defend yourself if need be.”

“But I have all of you,” I said, instantly hating the weakness that laced my words as I said them.

“You have us, and I feel that is all you’ll need when it comes down to it,” Magni said, “but we all agreed we need to prepare you for the worst.”

Dagr began explaining his technique, his fingers gliding over the wood, string, and arrowhead, pointing at different parts as he described their function and demonstrated how to stand and release.

“You sure you don’t want one of us teaching her the way to handle a bow, old man?” Tore teased from afar. The other huntsmen laughed.

"Someone who can actually aim and *hit* a boar, should be the one," Dagr said with a glare.

"It really should be me teaching Snow since we all know that I am by far the best," Freyr teased.

Dagr chose to ignore the playful jabs and comments in good humor coming from the other huntsmen as he stood behind me, his hands on my hips as he guided me into position at right angles to the target trees. He nocked an arrow just below the bead, and helped me to draw the string back fully to the anchor point. His arms were around me, distracting me, though I knew I should try to ignore the close proximity and focus on the task at hand. His breath was warm on my neck, and the sinful thoughts flooding through me were making this lesson far harder than he knew.

"Relax. Archery has more in common with art than war. It is a dance between you, your target, and the tools in your hands. Feel the breeze in your hair. Where is it coming from? How will it affect the arrow's flight path? Breathe in; breathe out. Hold your back straight, keep your posture tall, proud, as if you had a crown on your head," Jerrik said as he stood the closest to Dagr and me, watching closely as if to assure Dagr was indeed doing a good job with the lesson.

His words floated around me, embracing me. Under Dagr's guidance, I sighted the arrow and relaxed my fingers. The string snapped, striking my skin in a surprising fashion. The arrow flew with only a slight waver, striking the nearer tree at its base.

"Very good," Odin ordered as he walked to the arrow to examine it closer. "Again."

Dagr stepped back, guiding me to nock the next arrow on my own. His face beamed with pride.

I released five more arrows, before Jerrik and Dagr led me over to view the targets. Arrows stuck out from the base of the trees, having made contact each time.

"You have great aim, lass," Magni praised. "You're a natural."

"We should have her doing the hunting over some of you fools," Tore said with a chuckle.

I liked pleasing them. "Thank you." I smiled, feeling a real sense of pride.

Freyr's expression grew serious. "The queen is coming."

"And she wants me dead?" I knew the answer to this, but for some reason I needed to hear one of the huntsmen say it. I needed to hear the harsh words to keep me grounded in reality, to remind me that my life was not a safe little haven guarded by my seven protectors.

"We worried this day would come," Steen said from behind me. "But we will be ready when it does."

"That's enough learning for one day," Freyr announced, breaking me from my own fearful thoughts. "I'm hungry."

"I have rabbit stew cooking," I said proudly. It had taken me all morning to prepare, and though I still struggled in almost every aspect of doing it, I felt as if maybe I had finally gotten a handle on this wretched task called cooking.

Dagr took the bow out of my hands. "Well then, let's go try this stew of yours," he said with a small smirk that seemed as if he was in on some secret I was unaware of.

"Oh yes, let's," Freyr mumbled, as Steen elbowed him in the ribcage and shot him a warning look.

I'm sure they all expected a meal that was far from a pleasant feast, but I was confident I would surprise them all with my rabbit stew.

As we walked back into the house, the aroma of the stew wasn't exactly as I had expected it to smell like. In fact, it was the complete opposite. I wasn't sure what boiled human head smelled like, but if it had an odor, I was sure this rabbit stew would match it in comparison. Cringing as I walked to the boiling pot, I took a ladle and stirred the meat and potatoes around which only made the pungent fragrance emerge all the more intense...and awful.

"Mmm smells delicious," I heard Tore say from behind me.

His comment seemed odd because I thought the opposite, but maybe the smell of rabbit cooking was an acquired smell I wasn't used to.

"Well, it appears to be done," I said. "You can all grab a bowl if you would like."

"I can't wait," Freyr said as he was the first to grab a bowl as he winked at the other men.

Each huntsman followed Freyr and dished the stew into their bowls and sat at the long table looking at each other with wide grins.

"You first, brother," Steen said to Freyr.

"Oh no, let's leave that honor for the elder. Dagr can be the first," Freyr countered.

Dagr looked at me, at the bowl of stew, and then grumbled beneath his breath. “I would love to.”

He shoved a spoonful of rabbit meat into his mouth and slowly chewed, glaring at the other men as he did so.

“Well?” I asked, anxious to hear if I had redeemed my culinary skills. “How is it?”

He nodded and swallowed. “This is truly a meal I shouldn’t experience alone.”

Pride washed over me. I loved that I could provide a meal for these men, and though I may not be a fan of the smell, clearly Dagr was impressed enough to tell each of the men to dig in, which they all did.

“What seasonings did you use?” Tore asked with a full mouth.

“Oh just some herbs I found and some seeds.”

“Mustard seed?” Odin asked as he too swallowed the large mouthful of stew.

“Is that what it was?” I asked with a shrug. “I wasn’t sure but decided to put it in. Is it the seeds that make it so good?”

“Well, the seeds sure do give it bite,” Steen said,

stirring the stew around with his spoon, but when he saw me watching him, he was quick to take a spoonful and put it into his mouth.

"I have to confess," I said. "I was worried if I would ever be able to truly cook for you all. It seemed so daunting at first. But now that I can see how much you all like my stew, I will make it one of our regular meals."

"Oh good for us," Freyr said with a smirk which warranted another jab by his brother's arm I didn't understand, but brothers would be brothers.

"Aren't you going to eat?" Magni asked.

"Oh, I am not hungry," I said, yawning as I did so. "I'm actually a little tired and think I'll go upstairs to take a nap if you all don't mind."

Odin was the first to shoot out of his seat. "I'll take you," he announced loudly and with determination.

"Oh, you don't have to—"

"But I will. After all you have done for us—cooking this fine meal—it's the least I can do."

Before I could protest, Odin surprised me by lifting me into his arms and heading toward the stairs. The sound of the men chuckling had me turning my head to see the men emptying their bowls back into the pot of stew with large smiles and shaking heads. Right before reaching the stairs, Odin reached for a basket of apples and held them beneath me as he continued the ascent to his room. I got a glimpse of him glancing at the other huntsmen as he gave a mischievous wink.

Maybe I should have been offended that it was now quite obvious the huntsmen had, in fact, detested the stew, but the fact that they had all sat down and tried to act as if they were enjoying the rabbit disaster, said a lot for how they valued my feelings. These men truly...cared.

FOURTEEN

Odin placed the basket of apples on a tree trunk that served as a table by the bed.

"Sit on the bed, Snow."

I did as I was told. I had been with all the other huntsmen except for Odin. The others had pushed my endurance for both pain and pleasure. I had to admit I was curious to see if Odin, the shyest of them all, would do the same.

I watched as he took out a long, vicious looking knife. After selecting one perfect red apple, he slowly began to cut it in half. The knife sliced through the crisp white pulp of the apple over and over again, methodically cutting it into slices.

Holding the blade of the knife up to my lips, one

perfect apple slice clinging to its sharp metal surface, he said, "Take a bite."

Holding his gaze, I leaned forward and wrapped my lips around the apple slice, careful to avoid the edge of the blade. The sweet tart flavor made my cheeks and tongue tingle.

"Do you want me to take off my clothes?" I whispered.

"Yes."

Odin crossed the room and sat on a nearby chair, watching me as I rose up on my knees on the bed. Keeping my eyes on him, I slowly unbuttoned my vest. Tossing the garment aside, I slipped the thin linen shirt over my head. I gloried in how his eyes darkened and his hand paused halfway to his mouth with an apple slice of his own. Feeling emboldened, I cupped my breasts and dug my fingers into the soft flesh. They felt heavy and swollen, the rough contact of my own hands making me moan.

Standing, I slipped off my slippers and then removed my skirt.

My momentary courage faltered as I stood before him naked and vulnerable.

"Crawl to me," he commanded, his voice low and husky.

After a moment's hesitation, I fell to all fours. Wincing as my knees pressed against the hard floor, I slowly crawled across the room. Positioned between his open legs, I waited for his next command. He held the knife to my lips again. I took the sweet slice of fruit.

Odin then reached into his trousers and pulled free his massive shaft. I fell back on my ankles as I took in the length and breadth of him.

"Open your mouth," he commanded.

Squeezing my lips tight, I shook my head no as I fell back further.

Odin's arm snatched me back by my hair. "Open your mouth."

Gone was the sweet and bashful man. His authoritative tone showed me he would tolerate no disobedience. My lips trembled as I opened them.

"Wider," he demanded.

I opened them wider just as he pushed the head of his cock forward. Forcing the shaft straight to the back of my throat, my shoulders heaved as I gagged.

"Breathe through your nose."

Doing as I was told, I tried to calm my racing heart and rising panic as he used his grip on my hair to force my mouth up and down his shaft. Thinking to my time with Magni where I was forced to perform a similar act underwater, I tried to concentrate on holding my breath and relaxing my throat. Though I'd had others in my mouth, I had a feeling Odin, like Magni, was not going to be the least bit gentle.

The earthy taste of sweat and musk filled my mouth as his cock slid over my tongue. Unbidden, my tongue moved and swiped the underside of his shaft.

Each time he pulled my head forward, my body trembled as I tried to suppress my natural reaction to having something shoved deep in my throat. My fingernails dug into the soft skin of his inner thighs as I tried to push my head back.

"Lick the shaft. Get it nice and wet."

Since he had pulled free of my mouth, I gratefully did as I was told. Grasping the thick bottom half of his cock, wondering at how it could feel so soft yet hard at the same time, I ran my tongue up the length, swirling the tip over the sensitive head as I tasted his essence.

"Again. Nice and wet."

I licked and laved his shaft again till the skin glistened in the dim candlelight.

"Turn around. Put your face on the floor, and keep your ass high."

Obeying, I placed my heated cheek on the cool wood surface of the floor, nestling my bottom between his thighs.

The moment his large hands parted my bottom cheeks, I rose up on my hands. "Oh please! Please don't put it there! It hurts! I hate it there," I whined.

My outburst earned me a sharp spank on my right buttock.

"You will learn to like having a cock up your ass, Snow. Perhaps I shall discuss some training for you with the other men. Would you like to spend your day with a smooth wooden rod shoved in your ass to help you learn your place?"

Vigorously shaking my head no, I resumed my prone position on the floor.

I could feel the tip of his finger swirl around my

hidden entrance. My body clenched tight around it when he poked just the tip in.

"So responsive," he murmured.

Next, I felt the soft, large head of his cock. There was pressure, then nothing. Then more pressure. He kept pushing forward till my body relented. His cock slid in just past the head where my tight ring of muscle once more clenched down.

"Ow! Ow!" I winced.

Ignoring my pain, he repositioned his grip on my bottom and surged forward. My whole body rocked forward with surprise, tearing his cock from inside my body.

Before I could resume the position on my own, Odin grabbed me by the hair and pulled me back.

"I guess I will have to keep my grip on your hair to keep you still."

Now without pause or hesitation, he forced his cock into my tight hole, straight to the hilt.

I screamed out in pain.

"That is what you get when you don't stay in position."

"Oh god! Take it out! Take it out!" I pleaded.

His only answer was to pull back then thrust forward again. His fierce grip on my hair kept my body bowed and in position, primed for his pounding cock.

In and out.

Thrust after thrust.

Each new intrusion a sharp, cramping pain through my body. After several thrusts, it felt as if he were tearing the delicate skin of my body. Before I could protest, Odin pulled free. Using his grip on my hair, he swiveled me around to face him on my knees once more.

"Suck it."

"I...I can't...it's...it's been..."

"Suck it, or I fuck your ass dry."

"But it's been in...my...my bottom."

"Last chance to wet my cock, Snow," he warned.

With a whimper, I rose up on my knees. I opened my mouth then shied away, repulsed by the idea. Odin tugged on my hair, a silent threat. Licking my dry lips, I opened my mouth again. Squeezing my eyes shut, I hesitantly wrapped my lips around the head. My own musky essence was on the tip of my tongue.

"All the way down," he growled.

Choking back a sob, I lowered my head down over his cock, desperately trying to keep my tongue away from the thick shaft but failing. A final push from his hand on the back of my head had me swallowing it whole. After a moment, Odin pulled my head up.

"Now lick it. Lick the taste of your ass off my cock. Get it wet so I can fuck you again."

Tears trickled down my cheeks as I did as I was told. At first, I just used the barest tip of my tongue but that earned me a slap to the cheek. After that, I laved him eagerly with my whole tongue till his shaft was once again wet and ready to take me.

"Down on the floor," he commanded.

Once I was in position, with my bottom between his thighs, he placed his cock at my now sore, tight back entrance.

"This time, I want you to rock back."

"What?"

"Rock back. I want you to fuck your own ass on my cock."

"Please don't make me!"

"Do it now."

Shifting my hips back, I could feel his cock push inside me. Slowly, I moved till my bottom connected with his body. I had taken him to the hilt. I moved forward and gingerly repeated the motion. As I was concentrating on the task, I could feel Odin move his hand between my legs. The tips of his fingers began to tease my cunny.

"Faster," he barked.

Startled, I moved my hips back faster. I felt full and overwhelmed...dominated. The thought brought a wave of little shocks up my spine. I loathed to admit it, but I loved how these men used me, made me feel as though I was only a vessel for their cocks. A hole. It was so raw and primal. My wicked thoughts made me move faster, to tease the pain, relishing every clench and cramp.

Odin pulled my hair again. This time I knew my duty.

I swung around on my knees and eagerly swallowed his cock. Licking and sucking its length.

Tasting myself and him. All the while, my own hand reached down to rub my cunny, needing to feel the rising tingling pressure.

"I want your ass again," he moaned.

I turned and placed my cheek on the floor, submissive...subservient.

I gave a small yelp as he pushed his cock in. My bottom felt sore and swollen as he began to violently pound into my body.

It was twisted and wrong and I loved it. I wasn't bold enough to call out, but all I could hear in my head was a steady cadence...hurt me...hurt me... hurt me. Pain was real. It was raw. It was in the moment. The sick blend of pleasure and pain, pain and pleasure made me feel alive. It heated my skin, banished the cold, and set my world ablaze.

Each of these men in their own way had chased away my shadows and breathed life into my world.

His cock stretched my bottom hole. Just when I thought I couldn't take any more from him, I felt the flat of his palm on my ass cheek. The harsh sound of his slap resounded around the small chamber. Hot stinging heat crept over my skin.

"Yes!" I cried out without thinking.

Odin spanked me again and again. Each slap timed with his cock pushing as deep as possible into my tight, clenching passage. He fell to his knees, pushing me forward till my hips hit the floor. With his hands on either side of my shoulders, he thrust hard and deep. I could feel the scrape of his pants against the delicate, heated skin of my bottom. My mouth opened on a silent scream as my own release crashed over my body, seeming to rip and tear the pleasure from the grasp of pain.

Through the pounding heartbeat in my ears, I could hear Odin's roar as he pressed his hands against my lower back and released his seed deep inside my bottom.

For several minutes, the only sound in the room was our mingled harsh breathing.

Odin stirred. Sitting back on the chair, he grabbed my ankles and flipped me over till my back was on the floor, my legs high and open.

"Keep your legs open. Lift up your hips. I want to see your bottom hole."

Placing my hands on the floor on either side of my hips, I lifted them high, exposing myself to his lustful gaze. Odin reached to the side and picked up a slice of apple. Keeping his eyes on mine, he placed the thin wedge against my bottom hole. It felt cool and wet as he slid it up the crease and over my cunny.

"Come here."

I rose up on my elbows, then on my knees.

He held the slice of apple, dripping with his seed close to my lips.

"Open your mouth."

This time, I didn't hesitate. Opening my mouth, I let him place the apple on my tongue. Closing my lips, I relished the sweet and musky taste of our lovemaking.

Odin chuckled. "My god you are turning out to be quite the treasure, Snow."

Reaching down, he lifted me into his arms. There he cradled me for what seemed like hours, my head on his shoulder, lulled by the sound of his deep breaths. Sometime later, I felt him rise and walk to the bed. Placing me under the covers, he tucked in behind me. With his arm wrapped securely around my waist, I fell into a dreamless sleep.

FIFTEEN

Their only warning was the thunderous pounding of horse hooves. The huntsmen grabbed their bows and quivers shouting instructions and orders to one another.

Through the cacophony, I could hear repeated demands that I hide in the root cellar, that I seek safety. I couldn't move. The idea that these men were going out to face certain death for my sake stopped me stone cold. Our journey had begun as hunter and prey, with me as the prize. But it had changed. I felt it deep in my heart. I now craved their rough passion and protective embraces. After allowing myself to become numb and cold to the delights of the world, they had warmed me.

I now knew just how much they had risked to keep

me by their side. A queen's wrath. My stepmother's wrath.

The huntsmen had saved me more than once. I couldn't let them stand alone. I wasn't sure what I could do to protect them, but I was going to at least try.

I watched from behind the sacks of flour in the kitchen till they all bravely filed out to confront the queen. Keeping my body bent and low, away from the windows, I crept toward the door.

My stepmother was perched on a coal-black steed, dressed in purple robes with gold thread. The crown...my stolen crown...perched on her head. Surrounding her were over a hundred guardsmen, ready to do battle. Along the edges of the forest, behind the guardsmen's horses, I could see the villagers begin to gather out of morbid curiosity.

"You have betrayed me, huntsmen," charged the queen.

"And why does our queen think it so?" asked Dagr.

"The heart you presented to me, Snow's heart, the one I ate, was nothing more than a boar's heart," she said with a sneer.

My gut twisted at her hate-laced words. I had long

ago come to terms with my stepmother's desire to see me dead, but it was quite another thing to hear her utter the wish. I meant no more to her than a speck of dust on her boot—probably less.

"The queen wanted Snow away from the castle, gone from her life. We have provided that to you. There is no need for this," responded Tore.

"I decide what is needed, and I decide whether my wishes have been fulfilled. I wanted Snow dead," shouted the queen.

I watched as an air of unease swept over the increasing crowd of villagers. Apparently, my stepmother did not realize or care that she had a growing audience, that she was admitting to her subjects she had set out to kill their princess, the beloved daughter of their former king.

Magni stepped forward. "We will take Snow to a land far away. You have our word you will never set eyes on the lass again."

"No! That is not good enough. I want her dead! I want to eat her still warm heart," threatened the queen through clenched teeth as her eyes lit with an unholy fire.

"You get her over our dead bodies," roared Freyr as each of the huntsmen stepped back with their left foot to brace themselves for battle. Drawing their bows, they were prepared to battle over a hundred guardsmen to save me. It was certain death.

"So be it. Men, kill the huntsmen and burn the cabin down. But not before you bring me the dead body of Snow White."

"No!" I screamed as I came running out of the sanctuary of the cabin.

Ignoring the horrified looks of the huntsmen, I tried to break through their line and reach the queen.

"Take me! Take me! Don't kill them!" I screamed as I struggled to break Jerrik's hard grasp on my arm.

"Kill them all," ordered the queen.

Almost in slow motion, I watched as the guardsmen raised their bows. The queen's guard was notorious for poisoning the tips of their arrows. The huntsmen would be felled without a chance to truly fight. Breaking free of Jerrik's grasp, I dove in front of Dagr just as the first arrow was loosed in his direction.

The sharp point pierced my chest.

I could feel a cold, creeping blackness spread

across my body. The world around me tilted as all I could hear were garbled shouts and screams.

Then all went black.

❄

I FELT like I was underwater. I could hear sounds, but they were indistinct, muffled. As I swam to the surface, I could feel the warmth of a fire on my cheek. I also felt their presence. My huntsmen.

They were stroking my arms, my hair as they softly murmured.

Closer and closer to the surface I floated.

Their murmurings became more distinct. I could feel their anger, their sadness and pain. Instinctively, I knew it was over me.

"My lovely lass. We lost you too soon," whispered Magni.

"I will miss her laughter," said Freyr as he stroked my hair.

"And her dreadful cooking. What I wouldn't give to eat one of the Snow's burnt biscuits again," responded Tore.

"The cabin won't feel the same without her

bundled up in one of our quilts, her little toes peeking out," said Steen, his voice tight with emotion.

"Our beds will feel empty. No one will ever replace our Snow." Odin's sadness was palpable.

"At least her soul can rest in peace knowing we have avenged her. That wretched queen paid the ultimate price for hurting our Snow," said Jerrik heatedly.

"My deepest regret is we never told her we loved her. We should have done so, men. We should have told her every day the moment she opened her eyes that she was loved." This from Dagr, the hardest and most distant of my men.

My lips were softly pressed by each and every one of them. A soft kiss of goodbye as they each whispered in my ear how much they loved me.

A tear slipped from the corner of my eye to trace a wet path down my cheek. My eyes fluttered open.

I had broken free of the poisoned trance.

Staring into their astonished gazes, I smiled. "I love each and every one of you. I love you all. My brave and wonderful seven huntsmen."

EPILOGUE

T*wo years later.*

I SAT in the warm sunshine, rocking back and forth, holding my precious bundle in my arms. The day I gave birth to our daughter was the happiest of my life. My huntsmen could not have been prouder papas, each declaring the babe had her mother's fair skin, red lips and silky ebony hair. With my stepmother's demise, my first act as the new queen was to abolish the monarchy. I wanted everyone to live in freedom and peace without having to fear the whims of a king or queen. Besides, I wanted nothing more than to return to my life with the huntsmen in our cozy cabin.

Every moment of my life, they made sure I felt happy, safe and warm. Each day was filled with passion, laughter and, yes, still the occasional punishment when I felt the need to tease and stir them up a bit. And now with the birth of my daughter, I was happy beyond measure.

Leaning forward, I gave her a kiss on her soft forehead and began to recite my favorite fairytale—the story of how I met my huntsmen. Of course, I had to fib a bit on some of the details.

“Snow White gazed upon the seven dwarfs. Delighting in their antics as they each introduced themselves. Happy, Grumpy, Sleepy, Doc, Bashful, Dopey and Sneezy.”

“You are definitely Dopey,” laughed Magni as he punched Steen in the arm.

I looked up to see all seven of my men watching me rock their baby to sleep.

“Dagr has to be Grumpy!” piped in Tore.

“Come on, Snow. Tell us which one is which in your tale,” cajoled Steen.

I just smiled...and then stuck my tongue out at them, knowing my bit of spirited sass would get their attention.

"Looks like someone needs a little reminder on how to behave."

My stomach flipped in anticipation. I watched as the men discussed which of them would punish me. As they turned back to me, I could see Dagr rolling up his sleeves. My cheeks flamed knowing he was the one who won...also knowing what it would mean. Time spent as his hunting trophy, dangling from the antler chandelier while he pounded into my bottom, which was still sore from Freyr's attentions last night.

Tore took the babe from my arms just as Dagr flipped me over his shoulder.

Yes, I had certainly gotten my fairytale ending.

DARK FANTASY SERIES

GET THE ENTIRE SERIES NOW!

RED & THE WOLVES

QUEEN & THE KINGSMEN

Red & the Wolves

This is no fairytale...

As the Blood Moon rises, I've been chosen.

Chosen to serve, to obey...to die...for no one survives their time with the Wolves.

As I am dressed in the ceremonial Red Hood, all I can think of is escape.

But there is no escape.

The lives of my village depend on my submission to the accursed Wolves.

There are five of them.

Five men cursed to live as Wolves.

Cursed for generations, forced to protect my village from the dark forces.

But they demand a heavy price for their protection.
Me.

Five against one...against me alone.

My only hope for survival is to tame the wolves... but submission is not in my nature.

Queen & the Kingsmen

❄

This is no fairytale…

Captured and imprisoned.

They seek to break my curse by breaking me.

But I will not submit, no matter what tortures they have planned.

I am stronger then the Kingsmen.

Not just one man, but six.

For I am the powerful and feared evil queen.

My curse will stand.

ABOUT ZOE BLAKE

USA TODAY Bestselling Author in Dark Romance

We are all attracted to the forbidden. Addicted to the rush we get from reading something naughty...something kinky. We love to lose ourselves in the fantasy. The powerful lord who sweeps the lady away to his remote estate to ravish her. The cowboy who takes the sassy city girl over his knee to teach her a lesson. The devilishly charming pirate who seduces his beautiful captive.

I write those dark fantasies.

Check out Zoe's Website at www.zblakebooks.com

Facebook: www.facebook.com/zblakebooks

Twitter: @ZBlakebooks

Instagram: ZBlakebooks

ABOUT ALTA HENSLEY

USA TODAY Bestselling Author in Dark Romance

Alta Hensley is a USA TODAY bestselling author of hot, dark and dirty romance. She is also an Amazon Top 100 bestselling author. Being a multi-published author in the romance genre, Alta is known for her dark, gritty alpha heroes, sometimes sweet love stories, hot eroticism, and engaging tales of the constant struggle between dominance and submission.

Check out Alta's Website at www.altahensley.com

Facebook: facebook.com/AltaHensleyAuthor

Twitter: @AltaHensley

Instagram: AltaHensley

ALSO BY ZOE BLAKE

My Wantonly Wicked Reads

Papa's Prey

Trapped in a world of dark decadence, the innocent Corinne is now bound

to obey her new husband's every depraved desire.

Daddy's Home

He will make her pay for her past mistakes.

Dark Deception

He will have her on her knees, begging for forgiveness. It's time she learned why they call him, Paine.

Defying Him

The harder Phoebe fights him, the more determined Michael becomes to bend her to his will.

For more of my books check out my Amazon Page!

http://amzn.to/2FEpFsn

ALSO BY ALTA HENSLEY

Scoundrels & Scotch

I'll stop at nothing to own her.

I'm a collector of dolls.

All kinds of dolls.

Villains & Vodka

The name Harley Crow is one to be feared.

I am an assassin.

A killer.

The villain.

Bastards & Whiskey

Sipping on whiskey, smoking cigars, and conducting multi-million dollar deals in our own personal playground of indulgence, there isn't anything I can't have... and that includes HER. I can also have HER if I want.

And I want.

Captive Vow

I take you.

To honor and obey.

Till death do us part.

This is my solemn vow.

I am his.

Captive ever after...

Delicate Scars

I was delicate.

He was scarred.

But together...together we became delicate scars.

For more of my books check out my Amazon Page!

http://amzn.to/2CTmeen

Printed in Great Britain
by Amazon

44292952R00113